No Second Chance for a Cowboy

Escape to Cowboy Crossing
Book 3

By Alexa Verde

Dedication

Dedicated to Rachel M. The kindness of your heart has no limit, and the beauty of your soul has no comparison. Thank you so much for your compassion. You're a bright star to those blessed to know you. Keep on shining.

Chapter One

THESE DAYS ALONE in the large empty lodge were taking their toll on Madeline.

The wedding, as hasty and disastrous as it was, had been beautiful in its simplicity with a touch of chaos that suited Paisley somehow. How Paisley and Cormac's family had managed to pull it off was beyond Madeline. When she'd gotten married, she'd spent six months painstakingly planning and organizing her wedding to the minutest detail, and had changed her mind many times. She'd driven the girls crazy since her then-fiancé didn't want to participate in preparations much. She'd wanted it to be perfect, from white roses to elegant gold-embossed invitations. Yet her marriage had ended in heartbreak when her darling husband organized a burglary of their home.

A knife turned in her heart. Had he simply asked for a divorce, she'd have given him one, and the expensive house, paintings, statues, everything. Just like her ex, the house had seemed perfect and elegant on the outside but lacked love inside, only she'd understood it too late. She'd sold the house and all inside later anyway and donated funds to Paisley's project, unable to stay in a place covered with her own blood, where the walls seemed permeated with tiny molecules of her horror.

But he'd chosen the ultimate betrayal. She shuddered at the memory of lying on the cold floor, suffocating, gagging, bleeding.... Shivering, she rubbed her hands over her forearms, suddenly cold in a warm lodge. She'd been sure she was going to die like her parents had. Well, maybe slower.

Stop.

She shuddered again. She was going to have nightmares again if she didn't stop thinking like this.

Paisley's wedding didn't have the chic elegance Madeline's had, but it was... better somehow. More real? Hers was just... glitter. However, she could've lived without having her hair set on fire. If Brandon hadn't saved her... She grimaced. She didn't want to think about what could've happened then.

And she didn't want to think about Brandon because it created so many feelings she didn't know what to do with. And no, she hadn't stayed in Cowboy Crossing because she hoped to fix her relationship with him.

Totally, completely, and absolutely not.

Hmm. There'd even been a touch of mystery at Paisley's wedding with a butterfly necklace found on an empty chair after the wedding. Brand new and encrusted with small diamonds, the pendant sparkled in the spring sun. Madeline knew real diamonds when she saw them, and that jewelry must've cost a fortune. So far, no guest had claimed it.

Well, Paisley's eyes had sparkled even brighter than those diamonds when an intimate crowd, including all her foster sisters, saw her off at the airport. Their beautiful butterfly flew away. So very far away.

The loss squeezed at Madeline's heart.

She was happy for her friend and foster sister. Shining with a perennial sunshine and kindness she let others bask in, Paisley more than deserved all the happiness coming her way. Madeline just missed her so much already.

She'd never had a sunshine personality. Far from it. She'd earned the nickname Ice Queen in school for a reason.

So now what? She'd loved her job once, but doing autopsies lost its appeal. Paisley had gone to a military base across the ocean, and Arianna left to work on Paisley's project in Houston and keep an eye on the Wyatt mansion's inhabitants. Jessie lived at the ranch now, close to the lodge, and wanted to meet up soon. But she was a newlywed and should be spending time with her husband and his family. Back from their honeymoon, they were busy decorating his place to her taste.

Madeline had another reason for not wanting to see Jessie soon. Jessie seemed to think Madeline and Brandon should get back together. Her pulse increased at the thought. As if it could be so simple. Her stomach tightened.

Why did she have a penchant for hurting people she cared about the most?

Rusty walked toward her and placed his head on her lap. Her German shepherd knew when she needed support. She squared her shoulders. She considered herself a self-sufficient woman who didn't sit around moping.

She thought about taking him to the park, but she'd just taken him for a walk. Besides, as distracted as she was right now, she might lose him again.

But fresh air should do her good. She hoped.

Fresh air was the entire reason she was going to the park right now, and not because Brandon had helped her search for Rusty as if Brandon still had feelings for her.

Minutes later, she pulled into the small parking lot. She found the map online and studied it for the least-visited part. She wanted to be alone. She even left Rusty at home. No replays of the last time she brought him here, when he'd run off.

The ground was dry, so thankfully her heels didn't sink in this time. Though admittedly, shoes with high heels weren't the best footwear for a nature walk. She breathed in fresh air scented with foliage and grass. She hoped the birds' chirruping could distract her, but it was eerily quiet.

How did Paisley do it? How did she find joy in every moment? Madeline leaned to pluck a small flower, intent to see beauty in tiny petals. A branch snapped behind her. A chill traveled down her spine. Wasn't... she alone here?

Then pain erupted in her skull, and she saw bright lights. She staggered, her limbs suddenly weak and not wanting to obey her, her entire body becoming limp. She wanted to scream, but no sound left her lungs. Then the world went black.

Brandon O'Neill stopped his truck near the park, turned off the motor, and passed a hand over the thick hair he'd had cut into a ridiculous fade to impress Madeline.

For a few moments, he sat in silence. He needed to be alone and away from the ranch right now. As much as he loved his brothers, he'd been snapping at them. And while he hadn't been snapping at the horses, he'd been sulking so much they'd begun to neigh nervously and swish their tails every time he entered the stable or approached the field.

He always had plenty of paperwork to catch up on while managing the ranch, but he couldn't concentrate on pages and numbers. As he'd looked at the computer screen, he only saw Madeline's beautiful face. And it wasn't like he could show up scowling for his volunteer work with troubled teens.

This wouldn't do.

However, nature could often soothe him. He left the truck and breathed a lungful of fresh air tinted with scents of spring grass and foliage as he strode to the loneliest part of the park, away from the children or pet areas.

Once there, he ran his fingers along the rough surface of the oak bark.

He didn't want to be this way. Soon he wouldn't need to walk away from people or horses. They'd walk away from him. He should pray. But even praying was difficult after Madeline had broken up with him. Ripped his heart out, really, and he still didn't know why.

She'd warned him she had the reputation of a heartbreaker. Was that all there was to it? That she left broken hearts everywhere she'd gone, including his? Something cold squeezed his chest painfully.

Or was this his punishment for falling for a nonbeliever? He should've resisted his attraction while he'd done his best to help her.

Forgive me, Lord.

The cold fist hardened in his chest. Why did his thoughts always keep coming to her? Maybe because she stayed in the area. He'd had to be in not just one but two weddings with her because his brothers just had to marry her foster sisters.

Seriously, what were the odds?

When he ran into her in a grocery store, she'd glared at him as if he'd broken her heart and not the other way around. He barely resisted the urge to gnash his teeth. Oh, and this took the cake. Mom now invited Madeline to family dinners, and Madeline had the gall to show up. Mom had this idea that he and Madeline should get together again. Brandon would rather get his teeth pulled out without anesthesia.

Couldn't be worse than getting his heart ripped out without anesthesia.

Maybe if Madeline left Cowboy Crossing, he could start healing. She just... just irritated him. Her foster sister Jessie, now married to his brother, had let it slip that Madeline had the nickname Ice Queen in high school. No kidding.

The standoffish woman clearly had no regard for others' feelings. How he'd managed to fall for her in such a short time was beyond him. Yes, she was beautiful with large blue eyes, porcelain skin, and luscious chestnut hair, but he wasn't superficial. He hoped he wasn't.

Instead, the sadness in her eyes had drawn him in until he'd ached to make her happy, to know what made her sad, to carry her burdens with her. She had a combination of strength and confidence, at odds with the vulnerability he'd glimpsed in those eyes. Or had he imagined the latter?

In their small town, she was like no one he'd met before. Maybe if he'd traveled the world like his youngest brother, he wouldn't be so defenseless against this onslaught of feelings the sophisticated beauty created. In high heels and stunning difficult-to-miss dresses, mostly of startling reds or blues, tall and slender, she was striking, especially to a cowboy whose idea of dressing up was putting on jeans without mud on them.

Hmm, yes, she was sophisticated, and yet he'd sensed an almost childlike desire to be liked, hidden so deep under the layers of polish and elegance that he'd almost missed it.

Or had he been kidding himself all this time? Taking care of her after the car accident while she'd had her wrist broken and been helpless to do many things had awakened his protective instincts. Her tragic childhood history spurred his compassion. Despite her outward arrogance, she'd needed his help, even more so because she hadn't allowed many people to help her. And he'd needed to be needed.

Was that the main reason for the attraction? He *always* needed to be needed. Since being a little boy, he'd found his parents' approval when he'd done something kind to his brothers or animals, and it had filled him with joy. Maybe he'd projected his desire to be liked on her.

He'd painted his dream of her different from reality.

That she'd rejected him so thoroughly... scorned him so deeply...

Heat flared through him, and his fingers tightened into fists.

He'd been so wrong about that sadness—she *had* no emotions, no regard for his or anyone else's emotions, either. His rib cage constricted, and it took an effort to get another breath of fresh air tinted with the scent of spring grass and first flowers.

His parents had taught him to pray in difficult situations, even when it was hard to pray or especially then. He lifted his gaze to the bright blue sky.

Lord, please help me. I don't want to feel this way any longer. Please have Madeline leave so I don't get this... this irritation and anger every time I see her. Thank You, Lord.

He felt lighter after the prayer.

Then an inner nudge propelled him to move. The direction his legs had taken him surprised him. There wasn't even a trail there.

He pushed away tree branches.

Then his jaw slackened. In the clearing in the distance, Madeline leaned to pick a wildflower. With her gorgeous hair flowing over her shoulders, in a dreamy, teal-colored dress reaching her ankles, she was like a wildflower herself, as cliché as it sounded. The sight of her made his heart stutter, which irked him.

Yes, this was a small town, but did she have to show up where he went? This was supposed to be his place of solitude to recover from *her*.

A figure in a dark hoodie sprang up behind her and raised something large. A stone?

Brandon's blood went just as cold when he sprinted forward to stop that menacing person. If only he carried his weapon. He was a split second late as the person slammed the heavy thing on Madeline's head and she collapsed on the grass.

"Stop!" Brandon screamed as his legs pumped. Adrenaline surged in his veins.

The person in the hoodie and sunglasses took off in a run, keeping their head low, so Brandon couldn't see their face.

He had to decide whether to give chase or stay and help Madeline. The latter won.

Her eyes were closed as he knelt near her. He retrieved his phone and called 911, his hands surprisingly steady considering he was shaking inside. Now he regretted that this part of the park was deserted.

So he shouted, "Help!"

He slipped his hands under her head where she'd been hit and flinched at the feeling of something sticky. She was bleeding. He ripped off his jacket.

His earlier prayer slammed into him. He'd asked God for Madeline to leave, but he hadn't wanted *this*! She had to be alive. She had to!

When he felt a weak pulse on her neck, he nearly wept out his relief. But why wasn't she responding? He balled up his jacket and pressed it to her wound. The fabric was getting soaked through fast, and shivers tingled down his spine. Head injuries bled a lot. But what would happen if she lost too much blood?

He couldn't allow himself to think about that.

Head injuries could also be very dangerous, especially considering she'd lost consciousness.

Again, he shouted for help.

While he didn't want to scare the parents and children in the playground area, he needed someone to guide the paramedics to this location. Or should he carry her out to the parking lot? But would it be okay to move her, or was there a risk of further injury? His medical training was limited to taking care of his brothers' cuts and bruises and checking horses for obvious injuries.

The rustle of leaves made him look up.

Liberty Clark rushed to him with her adopted son in tow, and he explained the situation quickly. She'd grown up on the neighboring ranch and worked now as a veterinarian for their small town and nearby ranches.

"I'll guide the paramedics." Her lips set in a grim line. Then, with his thanks, she and her son disappeared among the trees.

Brandon sent up a desperate prayer.

"Please, please wake up," he whispered as he pressed the fabric against the gushing wound. He kept the pressure gentle in case Madeline had a skull fracture.

At least, she wasn't bleeding from her nose or ears, which would be a sign of a much more serious injury. He nearly buckled under the weight pressing on him.

Lord, when I asked to have her leave, I... I didn't mean it like this. Not like this. Please help her.

Out loud, hoping Madeline could somehow hear him, he said, "Please don't die. Please come back and irritate me. Make me angry. I can survive that. Please. Just... don't die."

Chapter Two

THE FIERCENESS OF Brandon's reaction should've surprised him, given his earlier thoughts and prayers, but he didn't have time to think about it. The wail of sirens played their sweet music to his ears.

Her eyelids fluttered and opened. His heart felt ready to stop as immense relief flooded him.

"Madeline, the paramedics are on the way. You're going to be all right." He stared into the blue eyes of the most gorgeous woman he'd ever seen.

She'd scoff at him now. For sure. But it was still better than her... her not existing.

The wailing sirens neared and then stopped which must mean the ambulance parked. The paramedics should be here shortly. *Thank You, God!*

She blinked, and those eyes clouded. "What happened? Who are you?"

Oh, wow. "You were hit on the head at the park. I'm Brandon." Was she pretending not to recognize him, or did she genuinely not remember?

"Brandon? And you are...?"

"What do you think, your boyfriend?" The scoffing words tumbled down before he could stop them.

He shouldn't fight with her now. But they'd often bickered, so it came naturally. And the stress of nearly losing her must've gotten to him. But before he could apologize, the paramedics rushed to them led by Liberty. Her green hair matched the leaves, and her strides were as fast and purposeful as the wind.

He stepped aside to let them do their job.

"I'll follow you to the hospital," he told the paramedics.

He'd call Jessie on the way on the hands-free phone. Jessie would be able to contact the rest of the foster sisters. Madeline would want to see her. Once the brief confusion settled, surely Madeline *wouldn't* want to see *him*.

He had to know how she was, so he'd go to the hospital. After he knew she was all right, he'd return home, and that'd be it.

He thanked Liberty for her help, and she left with her boy.

The police cruiser showed up. His cop brother, Ronan, who'd married Jessie, approached and winced as he clapped Brandon on the back. "Sorry. I was tied up with a three-car pileup right out of Cowboy Crossing. Of all times! Did you see the whole thing?"

Brandon grimaced. "Yes, but the attacker got away, and I didn't get a good look at him or her. Their clothes were baggy, and sunglasses and a hoodie partially covered their face. The person kept their head low. Slim build, almost skinny. Rather short."

Ronan patted him on the back. "It's still helpful, bro. I'll see if any footprints were left. Though I doubt it, considering we haven't had rain in a while. It would be great if a scrap of fabric got snagged on a branch. Did the perp take the assault weapon with him?"

Brandon nodded miserably.

"Okay, let's start from the beginning." Ronan switched from part-cop part-brother into complete-cop mode.

Brandon told him everything he could remember, reliving the horrifying moments.

Ronan took his statement, then started taking photos. "I'll process the scene, then go to the hospital to talk to Madeline."

"I'll meet you there."

Ronan raised an eyebrow, but he didn't say anything. Everyone in the family—pretty much everyone in their small town—knew the relationship between Brandon and Madeline was strained, to put it mildly.

Brandon wasn't going because he still had feelings for her. Because still having feelings for her would be ridiculous. "I just want to know she's okay. It's the right thing to do." He moved his blood-soaked jacket from one hand to the other.

His brother lifted his hands in a mocking surrender. "Hey, I didn't say anything."

Brandon hurried to his truck while Ronan stayed to process the crime scene and prevent its further contamination. By now, park visitors who'd heard the siren had gathered nearby. This was going to be the talk of the town for a while. Brandon grimaced as he gunned the engine.

As soon as he drove from the park, he called Jessie on the hands-free phone and told her what had happened. Like his brother, Jessie was a cop, but she worked in Springfield instead of Cowboy Crossing. Their small police department in town hadn't had any vacancies yet.

"Thank you for everything you've done. I'll be on the way to the hospital right now." As her voice came out tight and hard, he felt the same constriction in his chest.

"I'll meet you there," he said grudgingly, covering his worry.

There was a pause. "You're a great guy. Hopefully, Madeline will see that soon."

"I doubt that. I mean, the second part." But right now, it wasn't about his hurt feelings.

He floored the gas pedal, wishing he had the benefit of a siren. If he'd felt suffocated in the park, the cabin of the truck, while larger than that of the cars, made his lungs starve for oxygen. He refused to think it was because he was scared for Madeline.

He preferred the ranch's open spaces for a reason. One could breathe easily there. Except for... He pushed the thought away. While his passion wasn't exactly a dirty little secret, it didn't sit well with his upbringing. He was a cowboy, not a... Never mind.

He passed one car, then another, adrenaline pumping in his veins the way his foot on the gas pedal pumped more speed into the truck.

The road to the hospital never felt this long. He parked near the building and bolted inside. The hospital smelled of antiseptics and stale coffee, a familiar combo. Part of growing up on the ranch with five brothers was a lot of physical work outdoors and getting into mischief. The latter had resulted in cuts and bruises and occasional ER visits. However, this struck differently.

Well, he'd been here before when Madeline had gotten into a car accident after barely avoiding his horse standing in the middle of the road. She hadn't been used to the fact that horses could show up on the road, though usually, they stayed inside the fence. She'd ended up with some injuries, and his mother had sent him to help take care of her while she recovered. Considering it had been his horse and all. And man, Madeline had irritated him then!

But then, he'd also had so much fun teasing her. And it hadn't taken much to suspect the woman within her was one he wanted to know better, wanted to spend his life figuring out. She puzzled him even more than his attraction to her.

His rib cage tightened its grip around his heart as he glanced around the small waiting area with rows of navy-blue plastic chairs. He asked about

Madeline, and was told the doctor was with her in the ER now. She directed him to sit and wait.

Sit and wait?

His fists clenched and he paced the waiting room. How could he calmly sit and wait?

Before long, several of his neighbors turned up, as well as his parents. News here spread fast. His parents were always where they'd be needed, and he'd done his best to live up to that legacy. Warmth edged the worry. Life at the ranch was tough and busy, but Mom always found time for kindness.

She crossed to his side and held out a cup of coffee. "It's going to be all right. It has to be."

With gratitude, he accepted both the hot cup and her support. His gut still twisted, but he could get air into his lungs easier now. Mom always smelled like pies, even in a hospital.

His father didn't say anything, just patted him on the back, and that was enough. Dad wasn't back to his regular self yet, but he wasn't in the wheelchair any longer, a cane his companion these days.

A strong feeling of community, family, and love added to the many reasons Brandon had never left his childhood place. He had everything he needed right here. People he'd known all his life filed into the waiting area. Yup, when his mother started calling, people started coming. And for a reason unclear to him, his mother hadn't only claimed two of her daughters-in-law—Madeline's foster sisters—as her own. She claimed Madeline as if she were part of their family, as well.

Go figure.

One of those daughters-in-law was now in Germany with his brother who served in the military. But the other one, Jessie, still in her uniform, barged through the door, accompanied by her husband and another of their brothers, Kieran.

Jessie's gray eyes were huge. "Is she okay? Can I see her?"

"The doctor is treating her." Mom shoved a coffee into Jessie's hands. "Everyone, let's pray."

Brandon joined the prayer. Yes, Madeline had hurt him, but he wouldn't be his parents' son if he didn't wish her well.

After their prayer, Dr. McCormick walked into the waiting room. His gaze stopped on Brandon's mother as the authority figure, and he was right. Mom gestured for Brandon and Jessie to join her, then turned to Dr. McCormick. "What can you tell us about Madeline Wood, doctor?"

"There's no skull fracture and no damages that should affect Ms. Wood long-term." The words made Brandon breathe easier. "She lost some blood, so we're giving her a transfusion. We're running tests, including a CT scan. We'll keep her overnight for observation, considering she might have a concussion." He pressed his fingers against his temple as if fighting a headache of his own. "She has amnesia."

Brandon's forehead wrinkled. "Memory loss?"

Jessie gripped Brandon's arm. "So she won't be able to identify her attacker."

Dr. McCormick lowered his hand from his brow, his lips flattening. "I'm afraid not."

As her fingers cut into his arm, Brandon realized what her frown meant. If the attack wasn't random, it could be repeated. But either way, he doubted Madeline had seen the person.

While his chest swelled that Madeline was okay sans memory loss, his heartbeat kicked up like a horse given more room to run. She really hadn't remembered him. "How much does she remember?"

"Nothing at all before the hit on the head." The doctor's gaze stopped on him. "She's asking for you."

His jaw dropped. "Me?" He was her least favorite person in the world. Even if she couldn't remember him, surely she'd still *feel* that way. Sense something?

Jessie released her grip, then patted his arm. "She associates you with the person who saved her life. You must be her hero."

Huh? He blinked. "I'm no hero."

Dr. McCormick fixed a probing gaze on him. "She also says you're her boyfriend."

Several people gasped.

Riiight. Brandon grimaced and rubbed his jaw. "I don't know why I said it. It was sarcastic. It just... slipped."

The doctor's gaze turned pensive. "Ms. Wood went through a lot of turmoil. Her emotional state is fragile. Her memory might return, but she's confused and needs comfort. Right now, you're the only familiar face to her. Please be considerate of that."

Brandon's eyes widened as the words sank in. Was he... supposed to comfort her? The woman who'd ripped his heart up without a second thought?

"One of you can go visit her now. Now if you excuse me, I must go." The doctor hurried away.

"In other words, Brandon, you're her lifeline right now." Jessie sampled several sips of her coffee. "I'll do everything I can to help her, but you know what that means, right?"

All eyes were on him. He resisted the urge to step back. Instead, he clenched and unclenched his fists. "What exactly does that mean?"

Mom huffed, the gesture loud enough to attract his attention for her eye roll. "It means Madeline needs you."

That was what he'd thought before, but boy, was he mistaken.

"She hates me!" And that still hurt.

"She doesn't now." Mom pinned him with a stare.

His jaw slackened for the second time in a row. "But she *will* once she regains her memory." Just the thought stabbed him. And if he betrayed her by posing as something he wasn't, how would she handle that later? Besides, Madeline wasn't a Christian. How had his mother, who'd instilled Christian values in him, failed to remember that? Or had she hoped Brandon would somehow pass those values to Madeline?

If so, he'd failed.

"Until then, she'll need your support." Ronan wrapped his arm around his wife's shoulders. Great. Just whose side was his brother on?

"Think about it." Jessie's gray eyes turned pleading. This was unusual, considering she was so no-nonsense and rough around the edges. "Meanwhile, while I'd love to go see her, I don't want to confuse her further. It should be you to go see her right now."

And Brandon did want to see her, despite all the logic. His heartbeat increased. Hadn't his heart learned its lesson already?

Chapter Three

Brandon rubbed his thrumming temples, trying to absorb all that had happened so fast.

Jessie took a deep breath. "There's something else. I'll take care of Madeline's dog, but someone needs to help her while she recovers from memory loss. It's going to be difficult for her to navigate an unfamiliar world. It should be someone she's comfortable with."

Brandon's mother perked up. "She's welcome to move to the ranch."

"We appreciate the invitation. We really do. But it needs to be done in an environment more familiar to her. You know, to help her remember." Her shoulders sagged as she looked at her newlywed husband. "I'm sorry. I'll have to move back to the lodge with Madeline."

The misery rumpling his brother's face was indescribable.

"What about Brandon?" Mom offered.

Brandon winced. "What about me?"

Jessie brightened. Seriously?

Mom placed her hands on her hips. "I raised you better than to ask that question."

Right. Any struggle was futile when she was like that, but still... "Mom, surely you wouldn't want an unmarried couple living in the same house?"

"The lodge has plenty of rooms. Most have locks," Jessie chimed in, quite unhelpfully.

His mother tsked with a wave of her hand. "Well, it's progress that you see yourself and Madeline as a *couple*. But you don't have to move to the lodge. You just need to be by her side as much as possible. Now, go see her."

"Yes, ma'am. I'll go see her right now. But no promises to see her later though." It'd been best not to add that Madeline would never see herself and him as a couple. The thought stung.

Minutes later, he stood near her bed. His heart nearly broke at all the machines and lines, and the paleness of Madeline's face.

Compassion unraveled and grew fast. The former Madeline wouldn't be caught dead in a hospital gown. Her clothes had always been chic, and even a cowboy like him could guess the chic part. White gauze covered her usually luscious chestnut hair, now spilling beneath the bandage in a tangled mess. She looked fragile like a porcelain statuette balanced on the edge, about to be shattered. Making him want to catch her.

Yet she'd never looked more beautiful. Simply because she was still alive. He shuddered at the mere thought of nearly losing her.

Her eyelids fluttered. Even now, her eyes were the brightest shade of blue he'd ever seen. Even now, they made his pulse skyrocket.

Seeing her again was a bad idea. Such a bad idea.

A faint smile widened her lips, now lipstick free. He'd never seen her before without her trademark crimson lipstick.

"You're here," she whispered. Even her voice sounded broken.

It tugged at his heart. She'd always looked so put together.

He leaned closer. The antiseptic odor almost overwhelmed the light, lavender scent of her perfume, but a hint of it drifted to him. Her signature scent never failed to quicken his pulse. "Of course. There's no other place I'd rather be." Despite his earlier protests, that felt... true. "Not... not that I'd want to see you in the hospital."

"I understand." She chuckled, then coughed as if that had taken too much effort. Her lower lip trembled. "I–I don't remember anything. Or anyone."

His compassion grew. She'd always behaved like royalty. In a way, he missed that. He wanted her to be well. "It's only a matter of time. You'll remember." And the moment she did, he'd be out of her life.

Why had he submitted himself to this kind of torture?

"I don't like hospitals." Her voice was small. "When can you take me home?"

Even if she considered him her boyfriend, that didn't mean they lived together. Still, it was safe to promise, "Tomorrow. Hopefully, the doctor will release you tomorrow."

"Everything about my life is a blur." She sighed. "How... how am I going to reconstruct it?"

"We'll all help you. You've got foster sisters who love you. You've got my family."

"And I've got you." Her smile was unusually sweet.

His heart twisted. His darling relatives had a point. She was going to be confused and disoriented. The newlyweds needed to spend time together, and while the previous Madeline had been very capable and made it clear she didn't depend on other people, this injured and amnesiac Madeline shouldn't be left to her own devices.

"You've got me." For now. He'd figure out the rest later. But he'd be a fool to let her break his heart twice.

"Yes." Her smile widened. "You saved my life. You're my hero."

Embarrassment clutched his heart. "I'm no hero. Go to sleep. You need your rest." He did want her to rest, but a bit of selfishness spurred that request. He didn't want her to ask about their relationship. He didn't have it in him to pretend she hadn't ripped his heart apart by breaking up with him.

Her smile turned a tad coy. "Okay, but aren't you supposed to give me a kiss good night?"

This time it was he who started coughing. Right, boyfriends were supposed to do that.

He leaned to her, careful not to disturb any IVs. He only brushed his lips against hers, but even that was enough to make his pulse jump. Her eyelids fluttered closed, and tenderness spread through him.

She'd need someone she was comfortable with, and somehow, while she'd seemed to loathe him after their breakup, now he was the only person to bring her comfort. He was the person she admired, and boy, did it make him feel good, even if for the wrong reasons.

Bottom line—he couldn't walk away from her when she needed him. No matter how abruptly that could end. But what about her not being a Christian?

God would want Brandon to help her, right?

Just without falling for her again.

Lord, what should I do?

"I'm glad I remember you," she said with her eyes closed.

"You only remember the part after you got hit." He cringed. He'd better learn to think before he spoke.

"I could never forget you. It's not about your face or our history. I can forget who I am—well, I already did. And I can forget everything about my life. But I could never forget the way you made me feel."

Madeline felt disoriented in more senses than one.

She was supposed to know this place. She'd lived here for a while. But as she stepped inside the lodge the next day, her gut tightened even as a banner in the hall and balloons welcomed her home. The place smelled pleasantly of freshly baked pies and freshly picked flowers. A bluish flower came to mind that she'd seen before. Lavender?

While she'd been outside on the porch she'd tried to place the scent of the grass and the sound of the birds chirruping in the trees, but it didn't unlock the key to the empty room now housing her memory.

Or was it the room that had been hiding lots of skeletons?

She swallowed hard, recalling the moments of uncomfortable silence from several people who knew her when she'd asked about her parents and any living relatives. She had to rely on others to tell her who she was, and it weakened her in the knees.

What she'd found out so far about the murder of her parents and the betrayal of her ex-husband sent a shudder through her. Maybe some things were best not to remember. Maybe the key to her memory didn't click because it would unlock something too horrible.

Everything else she'd been learning like a child. Brandon had stayed by her side at the hospital most of the time, showing her videos on his phone and explaining what everything was. She'd been learning the sounds, the smells, and the images anew, and the sensory flood had made her dizzy.

Even dizzier than the hit on the head had.

The only familiar, even if vaguely, part of her past was Brandon. His scent of hay and leather and musk wrapped her like a soft blanket, though she wished his large arms would wrap her in his embrace, too. Her heart gave a joyful jolt at the thought. There was something... something safe about his presence, and in her current chaos, she craved that safety more than air.

Everything was shaky and wobbly, but he was steady and safe. No wonder he was a ranch manager. He had that kind of quiet command about him. Without saying a word, just by being there, he soothed her frayed nerves.

She sent him a thankful glance as he opened the door for her and disabled the alarm after they stepped inside. He was her rock right now, and a wave of gratitude spread through her.

A German shepherd shot out to her, and Madeline screamed. Her insides shook at the large, sharp teeth, the primal fear cautioning to danger.

Brandon stepped in front of her. "Rusty, sit!"

Rusty broke his run by using his paws and sat on the hardwood floor with a reproachful look of hurt.

"It's okay. It's okay." Brandon touched her forearm, calming her.

She took a few hungry breaths, finding strength in him once more. He'd shown her the photos of her German shepherd on her phone, so she should've been prepared. Her reaction was pure instinct.

Even if she wasn't familiar with her pet now, Rusty was familiar with her, and that guaranteed he wouldn't use those sharp teeth on her. Right? Besides, Brandon shielded her, just in case.

Her thudding heart took time to catch up to that thought. She remembered fear, though that memory was misplaced now.

"Would you like me to take Rusty to his room?" Brandon's voice was soft, patient.

How was she supposed to return to her life if she couldn't even pet her dog? With traditional black and rusty coloring, muscular body, and large intelligent eyes, Rusty was a gorgeous dog. His tail wagged, and his posture remained nonthreatening. He clearly recognized her.

"It's fine." Her smile wobbled. When Rusty approached her with caution this time and licked her hands, she took a deep breath and patted the rough fur.

"You're doing great." Brandon moved his fingers up and down her arms before releasing her.

Despite all the turmoil and confusion, a pleasant wave sluiced through her at his touch. "Thanks."

Rusty barked cheerfully, obviously relieved, then brought her a ball. Did he want to play?

"Would you like to go outside to the yard?" Brandon asked.

She wasn't sure whether he was asking Rusty or her, but she'd reply for both. "Okay."

The yard would be less personal than the lodge. Maybe easier to remember. And while she was sure Jessie, who'd been taking care of Rusty, had walked and fed him, the German shepherd had a lot of energy that needed to be spent. The fresh air should do them all good.

In the fenced-in and well-taken-care-of yard with lush grass, she threw the salad-colored ball, and the dog darted after it. He brought it back and placed it on the ground. She threw it again. The simple play calmed her somewhat, and she smiled up at Brandon. He smiled back, and joy bubbled through her. He had such a beautiful smile, open and sincere, and she touched his cheek near the trimmed beard as if reassuring herself he wouldn't disappear like her memories.

Images of a large bouquet of roses accompanied by a wonderful aroma flittered through her mind, then an image of a peach cobbler. But were they glimpses of lost memories, or were they her imagination based on photos shown to her? She'd had photos on her phone of the flowers the guys had given her, of the desserts she'd baked.

What was real and what, well, wasn't?

Brandon... He was real. She moved her fingers along his jaw, her pulse picking up. Then she leaned closer, clinging to him like a shipwreck survivor clung to the last debris floating on the water.

Emotion filled his eyes. "Madeline, I—"

Rusty brought the ball and barked, and she broke eye contact. She'd learned a lot of things in the last two days, cramming years of information into minutes. But even in that enormous quantity, two things essential for her survival stood out.

One—she'd had losses that could return to haunt her.

Two—she'd been blessed to have a man like Brandon in her life.

He played catch with her and Rusty until her arm started weighing a ton, and then she simply enjoyed the sight of him playing with Rusty. While she'd had only online videos to compare, it was clear Brandon was a great specimen of a man. But surely, she'd chosen him not only for the muscular body, broad shoulders, and tanned skin—all amplified by work outdoors. The kindness with which he'd treated her and Rusty was a precious gift not to be taken for granted. She'd seen him talk to his mother, who'd come to visit in the hospital, and the genuine affection there entranced Madeline.

Most likely, this juxtaposition of a large muscular body and the quiet gentleness he treated others with, as well as his willingness to help, had attracted her to him in the first place.

But the memory of the caring relationship between him and his mother—yes, that was a real memory because it had happened after the hit—caused her heart to constrict. Apparently, she'd lost her parents to a double homicide when she was seven, with the culprit never found. How can one miss someone they couldn't remember? Because she'd been so little when her mother had been killed, Madeline probably had only bits and pieces of memories about her even then.

The image of a peach cobbler appeared again, giving her a sweet taste in her mouth. So this must be a memory. Not only images edged the closed corners of her mind, but scents, tastes, and sounds.

Then she tried to place the scents in her present environment. "It smells like lavender here, right?"

"It's your favorite scent." He studied her as if she were his favorite thing in the world.

She was taken with him, but what *were* his feelings toward her? Her heart skipped a beat. He'd liked her enough to become her boyfriend, but just how deep did that attraction run?

She didn't like her desperation for that attraction to run deep.

Back to the present.

Huh. Interesting. "I like your scent more. Hay and leather. It's comforting. Thanks for being here. I... I'd be lost without you."

Did his ears turn pink? "Your foster sisters would've helped."

Foster sisters she didn't remember. Jessie and Arianna. Arianna had rushed to Cowboy Crossing as soon as she heard the news. They'd visited her in the hospital, but Madeline had felt awkward and disadvantaged.

Another foster sister, Genevieve, was going to come soon from Houston. Brandon's family had wanted to make a homecoming for her at the lodge after her hospital discharge, complete with pies and casseroles and music. The idea of a crowd of people she didn't remember in a place she didn't remember had sent Madeline into a defensive mode. She'd implored his family not to. They'd still left balloons and a banner and likely pies, though the people didn't show up.

Still disoriented, Madeline had asked her foster sisters to come to the lodge later, to give her time to adjust first. "I feel more comfortable with you. And you're my map to myself. To this house, too." She had no clue where anything was and hesitated to find out. The feeling of helplessness irked her as if it were an insect moving under her skin. "Sorry to be such a wreck."

"You're not a wreck. You're the most confident woman I've ever met."

Was she? She didn't feel confident now. But she appreciated his patience as he didn't push her to keep moving.

Something inside her shifted. She didn't want to be dependent on someone this much. She needed him more than he needed her, and the imbalance of power sent a warning jolt through her. As anger rose, she suppressed the sensation and made a few steps forward as if she were a child learning to walk. She nearly staggered.

What was wrong with her?

He wrapped his arm around her shoulder, steadying her once again. "How about you settle in the living room for now and I bring you a cup of tea?"

"Thank you."

He was so patient, so caring. She should be grateful, and she was. She could be navigating her past with only Rusty for company, and while she admired his athleticism, the German shepherd didn't seem like a big talker.

But a lot of things nagged her. The mystery of her past. The mystery of her attacker's identity and his or her motivation. The mystery of her parents' murder. The mystery of the depth of Brandon's feelings for her. The mystery of whether she liked tea. Too many mysteries, and she couldn't afford to be weak if she wanted to survive.

She squared her shoulders, resolved to solve those mysteries.

Somehow.

Chapter Four

GROGGY, MADELINE SCHLEPPED to the lodge kitchen in the morning, her mind in a haze for several reasons. *Wait a moment.* What was that smell?

Coffee.

Hold on. She didn't make coffee. She knew the scent, though. So she stopped in her tracks and tensed.

Well, a burglar wouldn't make himself comfortable in the lodge and brew coffee. She smelled freshly baked bread. And pastries.

Rusty met her in the hall, his tail wagging, and she leaned down and rubbed his back, grateful for the reassurance it brought. The tail wagging intensified. He barked cheerfully as if saying "Good morning."

"Good morning, Rusty." She smiled when he licked her hand. Did one talk to a dog? Well, why not?

Seeing him today was different. Comforting. He looked pleased with the back rub, but she probably needed this connection more than he did. He was a rescue, and the fact that someone would abandon such a great pet astounded her and twisted her gut. This unfamiliar world housed kind people like her foster sisters and Brandon and his family, but also not-so-kind people who abandoned and sometimes even abused their pets. She was unprepared to distinguish between the two. She wouldn't even recognize her attacker if she passed him or her on the street.

She needed to remember her responsibilities, though. "Do you need to go outside?" she asked Rusty.

Arianna, dressed in black pants and a black T-shirt, stepped from the kitchen. "Good morning. I already let him out and fed him. Gave him water, too."

Madeline should be counting her blessings instead of complaining about all the uncertainties. She had good friends. Was she as good a friend to them, though?

However, unlike with Brandon, who she missed with a surprising force already, a bit of awkwardness stiffened her when it came to Jessie and Arianna.

"Good morning. Thank you." Relaxing in the pleasantly rustic but spacious kitchen—all wood, which Brandon called knotty pine, offset by marbled gray countertops and stainless steel appliances—Madeline breathed deeply. Something about the place and its lack of pretenses soothed her.

Rusty stretched close to the front door as if it were his guard post, and maybe it was.

With that outfit, straight dark hair, and green eyes, Arianna resembled a panther. Madeline noted the observation with satisfaction. She knew who Arianna was now and what a panther looked like. For a brain that spent hours in confusion, that was an accomplishment.

At the same time, longing for Brandon stirred her. She couldn't expect him to spend time with her twenty-four seven, but he'd been such a huge part of her world since the attack—her entire world, really—that she longed for him with an overwhelming force.

Arianna raised her cup in a toast. "Rise and sunshine!"

Madeline felt like neither one as she plopped on the nearest chair, the cold wood warming beneath her.

As if understanding her without words, Arianna poured coffee into a delicate porcelain cup with a golden rim and brought it to the table.

Madeline took a sip and eyed the little thing with a critical gaze. "I don't think that's enough fuel."

"Oh. But that's the cup you usually use." Arianna studied her over the rim of her gigantic mug. That mug could probably fit in the entire coffee pot and then some. Now *that* was enough fuel to clear mind cobwebs.

"Okay." Madeline shrugged. Maybe she'd just pour several cups.

But not even an ocean of coffee would clear her lost memories. Her empty stomach tightened as she missed a large part of herself. Missed herself, period. She wanted to remember her time with her foster sisters and, even more, every joyful moment with Brandon.

The moment they'd met.

The first time her heart stuttered when he'd looked at her with interest.

Their first date.

Their first kiss.

People said nobody should live in the past. But those people hadn't been robbed of amazing moments they could relive again and again.

Then again, one should appreciate what they had now. And Arianna was there for her now. Arianna had dropped everything she'd been doing in

Houston and rushed across several states simply because Madeline needed her. Jessie would've done the same and moved to the lodge if Madeline hadn't stopped her. Genevieve and her daughter, Gold, were arriving in the afternoon. Paisley, their fifth foster sister who'd married Brandon's military brother—this was a small world indeed—now lived in Germany but called Madeline in the hospital a lot and volunteered to take the first flight.

The thoughts warmed her more than the coffee, and not only because the cup was ridiculously tiny.

While she mourned her losses, she needed to remember—right!—the things she had. The people for whom she was important. Brandon, his parents, her foster sisters.

Waking up and discovering she didn't have any blood family left was heart crushing. But somehow, she'd found a family of the heart, and she was grateful for that. It would've been so much more difficult to navigate an unknown world alone.

Maybe even impossible.

She traced a knot on the table's surface, enjoying the blots to its smooth polish as they added character and dimension. She had no clue what she was like, her flaws or dimensions beneath the smooth polishing. Was she kind, hardworking, intelligent, forgiving, caring? Or was she selfish and superficial? What things did she like? Though she had a good idea by now about the people she liked.

Sitting across from her in the breakfast nook, Arianna peered at her with a discomfiting intensity.

Madeline shivered beneath that unwavering green gaze. "Um, why are you staring at me?"

"Oops. I just never saw you like this. You usually style your hair in the morning and put on your makeup."

Huh. Madeline finished her cup in a few sips and got up for more. "Even if I'm just staying at home?"

"Yup."

"But why?"

Arianna blinked, breaking her intense gaze. "That's a good question." Then she slapped the wooden tabletop as she perked up. "You know what would cheer you up and maybe trigger your memory? Shopping."

Apparently, Madeline loved shopping. She crossed the kitchen, then brought her second cup of coffee to the table. "Right. It... should." Though she'd already discovered enough clothes in her closet to open a boutique. An insane amount of jewelry, too. Why would anyone need that much jewelry? Especially after moving to a small town? Surely, there weren't many parties in town.

Arianna pushed a plate with apple slices toward her. "Here. You love fruits for breakfast." Meanwhile, Arianna bit into a bear claw.

Madeline did her best not to salivate after the pastry. It could be worse. She could discover she was into celery sticks. Oh wait, that must be coming for lunch.

She munched on the apple slices, then moved on to peaches. The scent of peaches spread in the air, reminding her of something... or somebody?

"Uh-oh." Arianna looked at her phone screen after it beeped. "We got a visitor. Brandon. I'll buzz him in."

Madeline's heart skipped a beat, and then she froze. "Hold on. I need to brush my hair. And... change. And put on some makeup." Okay, maybe she could see the point of putting on makeup first thing in the morning. She wanted to look perfect for him.

While in her bedroom, her eyes popped—and not in the way she'd wanted—when she studied her makeup kit. No, *several* makeup kits.

Well, it shouldn't be too difficult to figure this out. After all, she'd graduated from medical school, and that couldn't have been easy. Several minutes later, she found her makeup perfect—*if* she was starring in a zombie movie.

Arianna strode into her room. "Guess who volunteered to go shopping with you?" Then she stopped in her tracks. "Um, would you like a little help?"

"I need *a lot* of help. I'm sure eventually it'll be like riding a bicycle, but right now, all I'm doing is leaving skid marks."

"Sure." Arianna picked up makeup remover and swiped Madeline's skin. "Let's start from the beginning. I'm much worse at this than you are, well, your usual self is. But I'll do my best."

True, the only makeup Arianna was wearing was some mascara and eyeliner. Heavy black combat boots near the door that must belong to her dwarfed Madeline's delicate sandals. If Arianna had lipstick, was it black, too?

Arianna started with foundation, then added a touch of light-blue eyeshadow and a pale blush.

Madeline smiled at someone fussing over her while a pleasant feeling curled up inside. While she couldn't remember her foster sisters, she sensed a bonding and trust already. The awkwardness was fading.

Then a thought made her sit up straighter. "Will Brandon wait this long?"

"Yes." Something unreadable flickered in Arianna's eyes. "He's a very patient man."

She said it in a weird way. As if... as if Brandon needed to be patient with Madeline. Or maybe Madeline just imagined that.

"You have excellent eyelashes, so you don't need mascara. Now, let's outline your lips. I'll need a pencil, lipstick, and lip gloss."

Madeline had no idea how many products went into creating attractive lips. But when Arianna reached for crimson lipstick, Madeline shook her head. "No, I'd prefer a pink one."

"O—okay. Let's start again."

Then Arianna brushed her hair. "Do you want it in elegant waves over your shoulders?"

"I don't want it falling into my face. How about a ponytail?"

Arianna coughed a little. "Sure."

When Madeline looked through the numerous dresses in her closet and rejected every one for being too, um, *dressy*, Arianna retreated to the hall. "Let me go talk to Brandon. Few men can be *that* patient."

Right. Madeline's heart squeezed. She chose designer jeans with sparkly buttons and silvery embroidery and an elegant turquoise top that should bring out her eyes.

Now on to shoes.

She groaned as she surveyed the plentiful rows. Why did she have to have this many choices? And why did all of them have to have high heels? Did she enjoy torturing herself?

She didn't want to make Brandon wait more than she already had, so she snatched the nearest ones, a pair of black pumps.

Okay, she could walk in them.

The moment she stepped out into the hall, both Brandon and Rusty stared at her.

"You look different," Brandon said at last.

Rusty barked, probably saying the same in his language.

Self-conscious, Madeline fumbled with the hem of her top, likely mussing it. "Good different or bad different?"

"Beautifully different," Brandon said.

Arianna chuckled. "Good answer."

The countryside on the way to Springfield was beautiful, all those sprawling hills and purple and white wildflowers. She didn't remember the flowers' names, or maybe she'd never bothered to ask. She was supposed to be a city girl, but the scenery spoke to her. She considered rolling down the window to see if she could breathe in the wildflower aroma. But it smelled of leather and hay inside the truck, a scent she'd learned to associate with Brandon, and she didn't want to lose it.

Her heart twisted. Was she needy? In the hospital, Arianna had let it slip that Madeline was fiercely independent. Did it irritate Brandon now that she was so dependent on him? Should she try to claim back her independence? Should she put some distance between them?

Or should she count her blessings, including this beautiful day with a great guy?

She turned to her boyfriend who was considerate enough to go shopping with her, though she imagined no man liked holding a woman's purse. "Thanks for doing this for me. Though I imagine you didn't volunteer."

"Well, sort of." He grinned at her before returning his attention to the road.

That smile made blossoms appear not only alongside the road but also in her heart. "Besides shopping, what other things do I like?"

"Jewelry. Going to a hairdresser's." His voice sounded a bit subdued as if he suspected she'd drag him to those places, too.

"How about something... I don't know, a little less shallow?"

"Oh, you were a great medical examiner in Houston."

"So I liked cutting into dead people." She imagined those cuts weren't shallow, so he'd answered her question there.

Chapter Five

MADELINE STILLED.

A memory of an unpleasant scent drifted to her. Could she name it? Yes, formalin. It was great to know that she was good at her job, but... Why had she chosen that profession? Why not a surgeon, like her father?

Would she ever know?

Something sharp, like a scalpel, sliced inside her at the memory of the sound of something shattering. Then came a loud yelling, but she couldn't remember the words. She realized what had caused that sharp pain. Guilt. But why?

Argh. A helpless feeling washed over her.

"You helped solve crimes and bring families closure." Brandon spoke quietly over the motor's roar as if he read her mind, bringing her to the present and offering a tidbit of comfort.

Her fingers tightened around the door handle, its smooth, cold surface another reminder of a scalpel. Only it didn't cut into her fingers.

Weird. A scalpel was used to operate on people, which she must've known since an early age. Why on earth would she want to cut it into her?

She sighed. "It's so frustrating not to remember."

"I understand." He reached for her hand.

She welcomed the physical contact, craving this reassurance. Especially after he hadn't kissed her last evening before he left the lodge. He hadn't kissed her when he came in today. She hadn't read too much into it then, but it struck her as odd now.

Was there some kind of rift between them before her amnesia? Or was he disappointed she didn't remember him—didn't remember and act like herself? Or that she was so needy? She shivered as if she'd stumbled down a cliff and he were her branch to hang on.

Or was he simply not that affectionate? Or was it she who wasn't affectionate? Was "fiercely independent" a sugarcoating of "cold and standoffish"?

She'd discover all that later. For now, she settled in to enjoy the ride and this time with him. Arianna had given them the names and addresses of the best dress shops in Springfield. Soon Madeline stared at all the mirrors and rows of fancy outfits. Was this her world? It didn't nudge any recognition, and it should have.

She spotted a few dresses in her size and picked them up. She didn't want him to wait long.

But she did want to look beautiful for him. Something inside her perked up. Okay, this shopping thing made more sense now. "I'll be right back." She hurried to the dressing room.

As she stared at herself in the dressing room mirror, a stranger looked back. A chill uncurled in her gut. It wasn't supposed to be like this.

Well, no time for a pity party. She shimmied into a crimson dress with spaghetti straps and smoothed down the front that fit her like a glove.

She walked out of the dressing room at the same time a tall blonde woman in the neighboring room did. The man waiting for her gaped at Madeline. The woman groaned and stormed back to the dressing room.

Brandon swallowed so hard his Adam's apple bobbed. Then he whispered, "You look stunning."

A rush of feminine power surged through her at the admiration in his eyes. Maybe she could understand why she liked shopping this much. "Thanks. Do you like the dress?"

"Yes." Closing his mouth, he tugged at his hair—a nervous gesture? But why? "But frankly, you'd make a potato sack look stunning."

Wow. He couldn't possibly mean that. But as she disappeared inside the dressing room again, she remembered she already had too many outfits in her closet.

Great outfits might help her be confident, but eventually, confidence had to come from within. She was told she had lots of confidence. She just needed to find it again. To find what she had a passion for. Well, besides Brandon. She couldn't cling to him like this dress clung to her, or she'd scare him away.

She changed back into her jeans and turquoise top, then left the dressing room. "I'm done here."

"Really?" His head jerked up, and his eyes lit.

"Yes."

She'd better not tell him how huge her collection of outfits already was. While her cop foster sister saved lives and her computer programmer foster sibling helped abused people, Madeline had collected expensive dresses and jewelry. That didn't sound like a meaningful life, at least, not after she'd quit her medical examiner job in Houston and moved to Cowboy Crossing. She winced at a slight sting.

The person in the mirror wasn't just a stranger. It was a stranger she didn't particularly like and probably wouldn't befriend if she met.

He offered to pay for the dress, but she had none of that. She had enough to pay for it. One nice surprise was her bank account. For a big spender, she had a healthy balance in her account, likely her half after selling her large house in Houston. Still, she couldn't be floating without purpose forever and needed to figure out what she was going to do for a living. Somehow, she suspected they didn't have a big demand for medical examiners in Cowboy Crossing.

Did she have any other skills or hidden talents that could be useful in a small town or on the ranch?

He opened the store door for her, and she took it as a sign of him being a gentleman and not of her being weak. His mother had told Madeline that looking after others was in Brandon's nature. Now that his younger brothers were all grown up and didn't need looking after, Brandon volunteered for a project for troubled teens at a neighboring ranch. While she was in the hospital, he'd told her about some of those teens, including Tommy, whose alcoholic father used to beat him up badly. Tommy had kept to himself at first but turned out to be a natural with horses, and after giving the teen a few riding lessons, Brandon even thought about preparing him to compete. Tommy had a clear talent. Though many teens in the program had the reputation of being runaways, none had tried to run away from Brandon yet.

Her purpose-free life seemed even more pathetic compared with his purpose-filled one.

"Thanks. Where to now?" she asked once outside. Sunshine caressed her skin, and she wished it was his fingers.

Why did it feel like something was off in the dynamic of their relationship? Not that she had anything to compare it to—well, anything beyond the romantic movie she and Brandon watched yesterday in the living room. There was lots of kissing in the movie and none in the living room, sadly.

He shifted from one foot to the other. "The hairdresser's?"

"You don't like the way my hair looks?" She grimaced while walking to his truck. Maybe the ponytail wasn't such a great idea. Besides, she had the urge to lean into him and have him run his fingers through her hair, which wouldn't be ideal with a ponytail.

"Of course, I do. You look gorgeous with any hairdo."

"Oh, good." Her stomach grumbled. Those apple slices didn't fill it. "How about an early lunch instead?"

He brightened as he opened the passenger door for her, but then his broad shoulders slumped. "There's that restaurant with French cuisine you liked. We could go there. Fair warning, though. Um, despite all your lessons, the only utensil I remember how to use there is the water glass. I don't want to embarrass you."

"Why would you ever embarrass me? I'm proud simply to walk by your side. Besides, considering I don't remember how to use any fancy utensils either, that makes two of us." She slid inside. The truck smelled of leather and hay, and the scent blanketed her with comfort. Huh. It seemed he'd sacrificed a lot to be part of her world. But had she done the same for him? "Is there a barbecue restaurant you like?"

Chicken wings. Her mouth watered. She remembered how they tasted, and now she wanted more to remember. Just like how she remembered the way his lips tasted from the time he'd kissed her in the hospital, and she wanted more.

What was she thinking? She'd resolved not to be clingy. Besides, if he wanted to take things slow, probably waiting for her to remember their relationship or become comfortable with him again, she could do that. No matter how much she ached for him to kiss her, to prove he was as attracted to her as she was to him. But without knowing their history, she couldn't take the first step, wobbling more than she'd wobbled on her high heels.

And she could only imagine what he must be feeling now. What would it be like to love someone who didn't remember why they loved you? Didn't remember your shared history and hopes and dreams?

He was selfless in not pushing her into more than he thought she was ready for.

He took the driver's seat. "Are you sure?"

"I want a place where we can eat food with our hands and lick our fingers."

He dropped the keys. By the time he picked them up and straightened out, the tips of his ears seemed pinkish again. "Sounds... sounds great."

He turned the key in the ignition. They made it to the restaurant fast, but his shoulders seemed tense as they walked to it. "I hope you won't be disappointed. It doesn't seem like... well, like your kind of place." A little grouchy, he bit off the ends of the words. Somehow, that sounded familiar.

"Then it might be time for me to discover new places and a new me." She hesitated before adding, "I feel like the me you know is a bit snobbish and stuck-up."

Was she going to learn things about herself she wasn't going to like? But he'd fallen in love with the her he knew. Would he be disappointed in the her she wanted to become? Should she try harder to understand and imitate the her she'd been?

It felt too complicated and treacherous, like she was a moth flying into a web. What she needed was clarity. She took a deep breath. Patience. She needed to be patient.

Then a disturbing thought wiggled into that web. Did she want him to like her so much that she'd be willing to change herself for him? No, that couldn't be right.

He opened the restaurant door for her, and the enticing scents of barbecue and french fries met her, filling her mouth with saliva. "You're not snobbish at all."

Great. That still left stuck-up. She marched inside.

"Wait. You're not *stuck-up*, either." He followed her fast. "Maybe a tiny bit. Just a tad. A little bit."

"I got it," she said over her shoulder. He'd protested too much, and that was an answer in itself. But, as much as it hurt to suspect he didn't like that part of her, maybe he wouldn't be upset if she didn't like that part of her, either.

But *was* she stuck-up, or did she project that kind of air? She was uncomfortable around people, and she'd attributed it to her memory loss. But what if she simply wasn't that sociable?

Frustration twisted her insides. More cobwebs to make her way through. Enough of self-searching, though.

Just enjoy lunch.

She shouldn't try to relive over three decades and figure out a multitude of things right here and now. She had to take it one day at a time, one tiny tidbit of recognition at a time.

They were seated fast. She fiddled with her napkin as she pondered this discovery about herself. Arianna had told her Madeline didn't let people close easily, which some people mistook for coldness. That Madeline liked things to be perfect.

Was this desire for perfection outside her way of coping with the mess inside her? She didn't know much about her childhood, but what she'd learned sounded painful and tragic. It must have left a trace on her.

"You're not upset, are you?" Brandon asked once the waitress took their orders and left them with menus.

"No. I want to know the truth about myself. And knowing it might help me change it." She attempted a smile. "I'm one of the rare people who gets to start from a clean slate." Unless he didn't want her to change? Would she lose him?

Stop it.

Maybe she'd best switch the topic. "If you weren't here right now, what would you be doing?"

"There's always a lot of work at the ranch. Feeding animals. Checking for any injuries or diseases and making sure they got all their vaccinations. Repairing equipment. Attending to the young. Mucking stables. Grooming horses. Tagging calves. Mending fences. And so much more."

Did she have any fences she needed to mend in her life? What people had she offended while trying to keep her perfect façade?

His face brightened. "I enjoy it, though I don't much enjoy all the paperwork that comes with managing the ranch. And I love working with teens at the nearby ranch who need a bit more caring and guidance in their lives." He paused as if he were going to say more but stopped himself.

Huh. Her curiosity piqued. Was there something he wasn't sharing with her? "Shouldn't there be a hobby? Something you do for yourself, not for others?"

He shrugged those broad shoulders. "Doing something for others brings me joy. So I sort of do it for myself, too."

He didn't answer her hobby question. Why keep it a secret? Or was he so busy he didn't have time for anything else?

"I can't imagine how you do it all. And I admire you for your kindness." She wanted to reach for his hand, but something stopped her. Maybe his lack of showing physical affection.

He cleared his throat as if her praise made him uncomfortable. "It's no big deal. God gave me many blessings, including a loving family, good health, and a ranch that is doing well enough. I'm just returning the kindness I received—though, with the way I can be grouchy sometimes, my family might disagree."

He showed that kindness with actions and not words, and that was even more admirable. And he wasn't grouchy with her so far.

"I'm far from perfect, but I do my best to lead the life God wanted me to lead," he added.

Did she believe in God? Did she pray? She'd heard his family praying for her in her hospital room, but she hadn't joined them.

Frustration struck again. "Do you know if I'm a Christian?"

His expression fell. "You didn't used to be. It would make me so happy if you accepted Christ in your life. But I don't want you to do it for me. It has to come from within. I'd love to share some literature and movies with you if you're okay with it."

She nodded. She wanted him to be happy with her, but he was right. This was too deep, too important not to come from within her.

The waitress brought their teas—yes, Madeline'd discovered *she* did like tea—and he ordered barbecue ribs while she went for chicken wings.

"Do you truly like it? Working at the ranch, I mean?" She studied him over the rim of her glass once the waitress left. While she was curious about herself, she was much more curious about him. He'd said he enjoyed it, but it sounded like such grueling work.

"I love it." His face lit up. "Besides, it's an important profession—feeding the country."

So he was one of those salt-of-the-earth hardworking cowboys. She'd chosen a great guy, though something still didn't sit well with that thought.

"That's good because the people of the country, especially yours truly, like to eat." Now her smile didn't take any effort.

He visibly swallowed. "I don't know if I should tell you this, but you usually don't eat much."

Her empty stomach nearly rolled over in protest. He'd better not try to stop her from enjoying her food. He didn't strike her as the type to nag a woman about her figure. Still, she raised her chin to let him know she wouldn't put up with any such hints. "Then today is going to be the first exception. Or maybe I'll make it a rule."

She took a sip of her cold drink, determined not to overthink his statement or let it irk her. Surely, he'd just been trying to be helpful, and she did have so much to learn. She wasn't just discovering herself. She was discovering him and his life. And considering she didn't have a job or any prospects of one and he'd said there'd always be a lot of work at the ranch... "How about I help you groom horses tomorrow?"

Maybe, just maybe, she also wanted to be a part of a world that included such great families as his.

He sputtered as he choked on his iced tea. Thankfully, he stopped coughing soon. "You—what?"

"Groom horses?" What was so strange with what she'd said? "I mean, I'm not offering to muck stables."

"If you did, I'd fall from the chair," he muttered.

Their food arrived then, saving her from commenting. Besides, talking about mucking stables wasn't the best lunch conversation.

He said grace, and she echoed with amen.

His eyebrows lifted, but he didn't say anything. Maybe he didn't need to. The way he lived his life set an example of how to be a Christian. He and his family must be people God loved a lot.

But so far, what she'd been learning about her life... Would God be disappointed in her? Was He already? God appreciated kind actions, not beautiful appearances, right? God knew how far from perfect she was.

Her stomach tightened.

Guilt. The echo of an angry male voice again. Now she could hear the words.

"You're such a disappointment!"

The sound of the door slammed in her face. She could nearly taste the saltiness of the tears running down her cheeks. But she couldn't remember anything else.

Her fingers tightened around the smooth, cold glass, and she fought a sudden urge to throw it against the wall and see it shatter. It wasn't supposed to be like this. She was supposed to get all her memories back, including the pleasant and joyful ones, not just frightening and confusing pieces.

Okay, enough.

She drank a bit of tea, then dug into her chicken wings with gusto. "I have nothing to compare to, but I think these are the best chicken wings I've ever had." As promised, she licked the sauce off her fingers.

His facial expression changed, but she couldn't identify what to. He gaped at her. Must be surprise.

"You don't like your barbecue ribs? You're welcome to share the food from my plate. And that's saying something because I *luuuv* these wings. May I share yours?" She stole a rib from his plate without waiting for an answer.

He seemed strangely tense.

"Mmm, these ribs aren't bad, either." She licked her fingers again.

He made a strangled sound, then emptied half of his glass. He must've been extremely thirsty.

She glanced around. "Why... why is everyone staring at me? Am I doing something wrong?" Maybe she should've used utensils, after all.

"Wherever we go, people stare at you, especially men. You're stunning."

"Okay, I like that answer." This time, she used a napkin to wipe her fingers. Everyone still stared. Weird. "Must be the burden of beauty."

"And now you sound like your previous self." He drank more of his tea.

Her previous self. The more she discovered about her, the less she liked her. And there was a bit of strange tension she didn't think should be between a boyfriend and girlfriend.

She didn't like the tension, so she'd better do something about it. She flicked a fry at him playfully. "Relax. Will you?"

He'd finally started on his ribs, which were yummy as she knew firsthand. Now, his eyes widened as if he didn't expect her to do something like that.

Did that stop her? No, she threw another fry at him, which he caught this time. At least, she hadn't dipped them in ketchup before throwing them. A thought needled. Someone she knew loved fries drenched in ketchup. But it disappeared like a mist.

Argh! She ground her teeth, desperate to remember. Or at least to forget that she couldn't remember.

So when he said "Payback time" and threw a fry at her, she caught it in her mouth. Based on his slackened jaw, she hadn't done anything like that before, either.

Could she make the best of a not-the-best situation? Could she try to rewrite her life? Or was she kidding herself? And if she tried, would she lose him?

Yet she giggled, then devoured more chicken wings. "I don't have much to compare to, but this is the best meal ever."

He grinned. "For me, too."

Maybe she wouldn't lose him. Maybe he loved her enough to love the new her, too.

At his response, joy bloomed inside her because he *did* have lots of meals to compare to. Her foster sisters said she could cook well, so her mind pictured a romantic meal she made, maybe near the lake at sunset. Or even at home. She just wanted to spend time with him.

Way too much for her liking. How could she learn to pull back?

His phone pinged with an incoming message, and she gestured for him to read it. "Might be from your family."

Even if she couldn't remember it, it was easy to see how close he was to his family. Envy stung. Her memories of her parents were most likely fuzzy even before the hit on the head. Or rather, in a red haze. Because they had been tinted in blood.

She grimaced, her giddy mood disappearing faster than her chicken wings had.

She'd been the only survivor that night. Her stomach, so full and content minutes ago, clenched. Did she deserve to be the one to survive? She'd done her research through her phone, laptop, and photo album. Her father was a brilliant surgeon. He could've saved so many lives had he lived. Her mother seemed well liked.

Granted, Madeline had been little that tragic night, but why hadn't she heard the intruder? She could've warned her parents then. Why hadn't she gotten help faster? Her father had bled to death before the ambulance arrived.

Maybe she was wrong to be so desperate to recall her past. Her mind might be protecting her from something terrifying. About others? Or about herself?

He frowned as he slipped the phone back into his pocket. "That was Ronan. He can't talk about an ongoing investigation, of course, but still, no leads on your attacker."

"It's no wonder, considering I didn't even see the guy." She thought a moment about the slim build and short height Brandon had mentioned because she'd been no help whatsoever there. "Or a woman, more likely."

"I did see the person, but I'm not much help." His frown deepened.

She did her best to lighten the mood. "Let's hope he—or she—just wanted to rob me. It's partly my fault. I mean, who wears diamond bracelets to a park?"

His frown ironed out a bit. "You do. High heels, too. You don't require any embellishments, though. You're a diamond yourself that always shines bright."

As his neck reddened, her chest expanded. She loved the compliment and even loved his slight embarrassment as if he wasn't used to complimenting women. He did make her feel special.

"I worry about your attacker coming back and finishing what he started." He drained the rest of his glass.

Her chest deflated as something cold squeezed her heart, but she tried to wave it off. "There will be no need for him to if I stop wearing expensive jewelry in public." She helped herself to another fry.

If he wasn't her boyfriend already, she'd worry that he stuck around mostly to protect her. Besides having a protective streak, he seemed to have an innate desire to be needed.

His eyes narrowed, and he leaned closer to her. "But what if robbery wasn't the motive?"

She placed the fry back on her plate as her throat closed. "Someone wanted to hurt me? Like who?"

"Maybe a rejected suitor?"

Something tight in his voice indicated he could imagine some guy getting hurt over her rejection. But surely, they'd been together long enough she hadn't rejected anyone *recently* to cause an attack. She needed to ask about their relationship, how and when they met, but such questions felt too… vulnerable.

Still, she pondered it. "Your brother asked that question, but as I didn't remember anything, Arianna and Jessie made a list they gave him. I believe it took his entire notebook. I don't know how I had time for a job with that many suitors."

Brandon looked like he ate something sour. Was it the lime in his tea? "Right. I think he's checking for any newcomers in town from gas station camera feeds and cross-referencing it with the list. Arianna said one of your former suitors, Jason Madris, threatened you, so Ronan is checking his whereabouts at the time of the attack. Now, what about former girlfriends of your suitors?"

The food hardened to a stone in her stomach. "I wouldn't steal someone's man!" At least, she hoped she wouldn't, considering she couldn't remember anything. She grimaced as she realized she shredded her napkin into tiny pieces.

"Some men volunteer to be stolen," he said quietly. "I'm sorry. I shouldn't have brought this up. It's causing you distress, and you don't remember the names, anyway."

A migraine started brewing in her temples. Maybe she didn't *want* to remember. Then she perked up. "Oh, on the bright side, what if the assault was connected with my old job? From what Jessie said, I helped to put several criminals away. At least some of them could be released by now and decide to seek revenge."

He stared at her. "You consider that a bright side?"

She took a long sip of her drink. "Better than thinking I stole someone's boyfriend."

"I'll talk to Ronan. If he didn't look at that angle, I'm sure he will now."

"Unless…" She went cold inside, and it had nothing to do with the cold glass in her hand. "No, it's too preposterous."

He leaned closer, a softness in his brown eyes. "Tell me. I want this solved as much as you do. Probably more."

Did he care about her that much? Or was he already getting tired of playing bodyguard?

She took another sip and thudded the glass back on the table. "In the hospital, Ronan asked me whether I thought it could be connected with my parents' murders." An icicle turned in her chest. "I didn't think so. Decades have passed. Why now? But what if I'm wrong?"

Was that it? Was the trace of tension emanating from him the result of his worry for her? Or was there something in their relationship he wasn't telling her?

Chapter Six

The next day, Brandon didn't believe Madeline was going to show up at the stable.

Seriously, she'd be afraid to break one of those long lavender-polished nails with their sparkly silver-dot embellishments, and manure didn't exactly smell like her favorite perfume.

He flicked his hair away from his eyes, snorting again at the foolishness of getting it cut like he had. He'd much rather be doing something useful than spending time before a mirror fixing up his hair the way the hairdresser had taught him to maintain the cut. What a waste of effort, especially once he put on a cowboy hat and smashed the whole thing. He'd never cared about such things before.

Of course, Madeline would think the opposite and much rather spend her time in front of the mirror primping.

He couldn't even picture her grooming horses. He was sure the horses couldn't, either. So he'd started without her.

However, he didn't have difficulty imagining *her*, though normally he was engrossed in his work. Her image stayed with him nearly all the time. Even in his dreams.

She seemed like a new person lately with a different personality, and if he didn't know any better, he'd suspect a twin switch. Nah, that was more the stuff from a romantic comedy, like the one he'd watched with her because she liked that stuff. He'd much rather watch a good ole Western. Though to be on the safe side, he'd confirmed with Jessie that Madeline, with absolute certainty, couldn't have a secret twin.

He liked this new Madeline way better. She was fun, considerate, and cheerful. She didn't care about appearances and laughed easily. He wanted her to stay this way. Though it wasn't... it wasn't like he wished she wouldn't regain her memory. He flinched, and Tempest lifted his head and neighed.

"Sorry, buddy." He patted the chestnut Thoroughbred's long neck, Tempest's magnificent coat smooth under his fingers.

Tempest was a rare beauty with a chiseled head, long legs, and lean, muscular body. High-spirited and fast, he displayed the stamina and speed typical for his breed. No wonder the breed held more world records than any others.

"How can I resist her?" Brandon asked Tempest.

The horse neighed as if he didn't know, either.

Brandon had once fallen in love with the woman he sensed within Madeline, a woman she'd only shown him glimpses of as she let him edge into her world and life. Now, that woman had opened the secret places of her soul to him and invited him in fully. He'd done his best not to take advantage of the situation and resisted hugging or kissing her, no matter how difficult that had been.

Beautiful Madeline with her standoffish personality was attractive. But beautiful Madeline with a fun personality was *irresistible*.

While she considered him her boyfriend, he knew he wasn't. It was torture to wait for the other high-heeled shoe to drop, for her to remember everything, including their breakup.

He started grooming Tempest, which he should be doing already instead of asking the horse for relationship advice.

But if she might be in danger, he couldn't walk away, even to protect his heart. The heart that fluttered even at the thought of her. The discovery that several people had threatened her surged his protective instincts into full gear, making them stand guard.

When she stepped inside the stable, bringing her signature lavender scent, he could barely believe his eyes. For several reasons. "You're here!"

"Well, yeah. I said I would be." She grinned and tugged on the sleeves of a Wrangler shirt that was too short for her and clearly borrowed, most likely from Jessie, who'd adjusted to ranch life well.

The jeans, however, fit Madeline well, but he moved his gaze quickly from her mile-long shapely legs. No wonder she used to work as a model.

Her cowboy boots had heels and zirconia studs and seemed to be designed more as a fashion statement than for ranch work. Her luscious hair hugged her shapely shoulders, creating an instant urge to feel its silky waves. Though now would be a good time to have it in a ponytail.

Brandon's brother Kieran walked in, looked at Madeline, said hi, picked up his jaw from the straw-covered floor, and left.

Yup, that was the way Brandon felt. Only he wasn't leaving.

She snugged her hair into a low ponytail. "So where do I start?"

A few horses neighed and swished their tails as if worried about her level of expertise. So he'd best start her with the calmest and most patient one.

He led her to a leopard Appaloosa. "This is Speckles."

"She's beautiful." Madeline stepped forward.

Speckles boasted a distinctive white coat with dark spots, striped hooves, and a deep chest. If Tempest had a temper, Speckles had a patient sweetness. She lifted her graceful neck and neighed, then swished her tail. Her ears pinned back, which wasn't a good sign. She might be feeling threatened, and that could make her act out despite her calm nature.

Brandon patted the Appaloosa's neck reassuringly while gesturing to Madeline to stay in place.

"First, let her get used to your scent. Second, horses have two blind spots. One is right in front of their eyes, and the second one is behind them. Please make sure you don't get behind the horse. She might kick you because she senses you and gets scared. Third, horses are prey animals and get spooked easily. Don't make sudden movements."

"Got it." Madeline extended her hand, her posture relaxed and open.

It must've affected Speckles because the mare stopped swishing her tail, and her ears took their usual position. He waited for any other signs of distress, and when she didn't display any, he gestured Madeline closer.

Madeline didn't rush but moved with her arms open and let Speckles sniff her. "I brought some carrots. Is it okay if I give them to her?"

He nodded in approval, and so did Speckles. "That was nice of you."

Madeline laughed as Speckles nibbled the carrots in her hand. "Speckles would be doing me a favor. Arianna said I had carrots for dinner sometimes." A quick grimace told him what Madeline now thought of that.

He brought the bucket with brushes and explained the order to use them in.

"Okay, thanks." She smiled.

His heart shifted. After amnesia, she smiled so much more, and her smiles were different. Before, her smiles had been careful as if she'd been afraid to be cheerful. Now, they stretched from ear to ear and brightened her entire face.

He should be working, but once again, he couldn't look away from her as she picked up the first brush and started cleaning Speckles's speckled coat. Even as she did a mundane job, something he'd done and seen done nearly every day of his life, her image begged to be turned into a painting.

If he'd ever seen God's masterpiece, Madeline was it.

He should tell her the truth about their breakup. Today. His stomach clenched at the thought of losing her, and a knife seemed to turn in his chest.

Her expression was tender as she whispered something to Speckles, then turned serious when she glanced back at him. "Ronan emailed me some information. The suitor who'd threatened me, Jason Madris, had an alibi for the time of my assault. The rest of my suitors will take a while to go through. But here's something. I told Ronan about my suspicions, and he found out that a man named Matt Luettgen was released two months ago on parole. He committed what the judge ruled as manslaughter. Apparently, I testified in court as an expert witness about the cause of death. It's a routine procedure, really. But Luettgen screamed obscenities that he was going to get back at me."

Everything inside him went into protective mode. It also put him into action, and he returned to grooming the Thoroughbred. "I assume this happened in Houston. Did he make contact with his parole officer after being released?"

Her mouth set in a tight line, but her brush strokes remained even. Shockingly, he felt more rattled than she looked.

But then, her emotions were never on the surface. "That's the thing. Luettgen went off the grid. Jessie contacted her friends in the Houston police department, and this is the info she received. He stayed with his uncle after his release, and the uncle gave him a job at his store. Three days ago, Luettgen left his uncle's house in the morning but didn't show up for work. His uncle's laptop, tablet, cash, and jewelry went missing."

"Can they track down the tablet with GPS?" Brandon had learned a thing or two from his cop brother, though Brandon still preferred working with horses.

"Both the laptop and tablet are turned off. I assume Luettgen took them as sources of fast cash." She looked away. "It doesn't mean he's headed here, though."

"You still should be careful." His rib cage constricted. The sense of heightened alert also meant he couldn't tell her about their breakup yet. If the assault in the park hadn't been a robbery, then her life might be in danger.

He was an honest guy, and this was the first time he'd lied to someone, even if he hadn't meant to.

Lord, please forgive me.

But how could Brandon tell her the truth if it could harm her? How did he get himself in this situation?

Maybe because part of him *wanted* to be in this situation, to have a second chance with her. No matter what he'd told himself, he'd never gotten over her. He'd have to guard his heart somehow while doing his best to keep her safe.

Yeah, easier said than done. He moved to the next horse. Best to keep working. Because looking at Madeline was too distracting. Even a simple outfit similar to the ones he saw around him daily looked so attractive on her it made his pulse stutter.

So much for guarding his heart.

"What about tracking his cell phone?" Despite his inner turmoil, he kept his voice even and confident for the horses' sake. They could pick up on emotional distress.

She sighed as she took another brush from the bucket. "He left it at his uncle's place. Probably already bought a burner by then."

"Can that uncle be trusted to tell the truth? Maybe he's covering for his nephew."

"Good question and one I don't have an answer to. Ronan and Jessie are looking into it."

Right. Too bad he didn't have their investigative skills.

Normally, Brandon was happy being a cowboy. Working at the ranch ran in his family's blood for generations. It was what he was born to do, what gave his life a purpose.

But could a sophisticated city beauty fall for a simple rancher? His gut tightened. Most likely, when she regained her memory, she'd leave for the big city lights with their fancy stores and operas and art galleries and whatever else they had.

Leaving him and his broken—again—heart behind.

He squared his shoulders. For Madeline, he'd have to take that risk. "If you see or sense any sign of danger, please let me know immediately."

She nodded without hesitation. "Of course."

He barely resisted the urge to draw her close. This Madeline was so different from the Madeline he'd known who'd constantly needed to assert her independence. This Madeline was still self-sufficient, but more approachable.

And that made it even more difficult not to fall for her.

The next day, Brandon stopped Madeline before she headed toward Dotty, grooming tools in her hand. "I'll take care of this horse myself."

Hurt flashed in Madeline's eyes, as if he didn't trust her with the horse's care. "You told me I did well yesterday."

"It's not that, and you did." He lowered his voice as if Dotty could overhear him. "I bought Dotty recently because her owner no longer wanted to take care of her. She is getting used to me, but she was under a lot of stress. A new person can frighten her."

Dotty was another Appaloosa, but unlike other horses of her breed, she wasn't currently friendly. He couldn't blame her. Although she looked better than when he'd bought her, she had a long way to go.

Madeline's eyes softened as she stepped close to him. "Ooooh. What's wrong with her? She's skinny, and her pretty spotted coat lacks luster... Is she sick?"

"She has an equine gastric ulcer." He approached Dotty with caution. He'd already given her omeprazole and pain medicine for her stomach. But by the looks of it, Dotty had suffered in silence for a long time, and that couldn't improve anyone's character. Ask him how he knew.

"Poor thing." Compassion coated Madeline's voice. "That must be painful."

He checked to make sure Dotty had continuous feed. She'd finally started eating, which was a good sign. "Sadly, ulcers are rather prevalent in horses. About ninety percent of horses might get them at some point in their lives. Their stomachs are small compared to their bodies, and acids can get splashed from the stomach's lower part that has a protective lining, to the upper part that doesn't. Then an equine gastric ulcer can form."

"Yikes." She started grooming Speckles, who was familiar with her now. "Does that mean a lot of your horses have ulcers?"

"No. We do our best to prevent them. We make sure our horses eat frequently or graze and turn them out to pasture a lot. We don't add lots of grain to their diet in winter, and so on. Stress can increase the likelihood of ulcers, so we make sure our horses feel safe and can see and hear each other at all times. We watch for signs of ulcers. The most telltale one is the horse stopping eating or drinking, but it can also be the horse standing with her legs wide apart, refusing to get trained, and so on. Sometimes they display colic-like symptoms." He patted Dotty before brushing her coat gently. Since she'd been neglected, he made sure to give her extra attention.

"How do you know for sure the cause is an ulcer and not something else?" She had such an inquisitive mind.

He liked that. But then, he liked way too many things about her. A ping of guilt reminded him he should be concentrating on Dotty, not Madeline. "In this case, Liberty did a gastroendoscopy after she examined her and gave her the necessary vaccines. That's when an endoscope is put through the horse's nostrils." He grimaced. "Sorry, Dotty."

But he should be grateful Dotty didn't have anything worse. He'd seen horses with a big array of diseases, had cared for them. It wasn't even that the people who'd had them were cruel. Like in the case with Dotty, they'd bought them for their children's entertainment and had no clue how to care for horses properly. And obviously, horses couldn't tell people when they were hurting and what place was hurting.

He stole a glance at Madeline again. Her brush strokes were smooth, and she and the Appaloosa were a vision to be seen, to be put on canvas. He couldn't wait....

Stop.

He had too many important things to do to waste time thinking about those that didn't give practical results.

"I'm amazed how much you care." Madeline's voice was as smooth as her strokes. He remembered the gentle way her fingertips touched his face when he'd brought her to the lodge from the hospital. She could be distant, but she could be so gentle, too. His pulse kicked up.

Concentrate.

He apologized to Dotty for a different reason as he attended to her coat. "I love what I'm doing. Horses are magnificent, incredible animals, but they are dependent on us to keep them well. I don't take that responsibility lightly." Then he stopped. "I must be boring you."

She shook her head. "I find your knowledge and attitude admirable."

Wow. She had intricate knowledge of how the human body worked, even if she didn't remember it right now, and she admired him for knowing about horse ulcers? Go figure.

And nobody before had accused him of having a good attitude. He loved the way she saw him now.

His heart shifted as he changed brushes. He couldn't let himself get addicted to this new version of her. He needed to take it in small doses, or the acid of her leaving later wouldn't just burn a hole in his stomach but in his entire life.

Again, easier said than done.

In the evening, they had dinner at his mother's place after Madeline made a dessert that melted in his mouth. When they checked on the horses after dinner, his heart fell at the sight of Dotty. She had her legs apart again and moved her head to the side. She looked uncomfortable. Was she in pain? Or was she experiencing some side effects from her medication?

Madeline turned to him, her gaze worried. "Should we call the vet?"

He nodded, thankful Liberty lived at the neighboring ranch and accepted calls after hours. She loved farm animals as much as he did, maybe even more. She showed up in no time. After examining Dotty, Liberty increased the dosage of painkillers slightly and asked him to monitor Dotty and call her if things got worse.

Madeline took the latter literally. "I'm staying here for the night," she said after Liberty left and he gave Dotty the medicine.

He gawked at her. "You're what?" That was like imagining a princess sleeping in the stable instead of, well, however many mattresses that princess in the fairy tale had been sleeping on.

"I want to make sure Dotty gets better."

"You don't have to stay here," he said.

She shook her head, and her ponytail bounced. "I want to."

Wow. She really cared about a horse she'd just met for the first time. Compassion filled those blue eyes that were often ice cold. "Same can be said about you. You don't have to stay here. I'll call you if there are any changes."

Was she serious?

His jaw dropped. This was his horse, his responsibility, his life. Instead, he simply repeated her words. "I want to."

He brought them chairs and blankets. Tenderness filled him when her head slipped to his shoulder.

Did she show her true self now, when she didn't realize she needed to protect something fragile inside her? Before the attack, she'd donned her immaculate makeup and fancy outfits like armor, in addition to her distant attitude. She was an enigma he couldn't decipher, no matter how much he'd tried. Maybe that was part of the attraction.

A question that worried him more was whether she'd revert to keeping everyone, including him, at arm's length once she regained her memories. Assuming she'd forgive him for not telling her about their breakup.

Argh.

"Look at the bright side," she said. "I'm sure no perp who knows anything about my life would look for me at the stable."

He wouldn't exactly call that a bright side, but she had a point.

An hour later, Liberty stopped by to check on the poor Appaloosa. Relief flooded Brandon, and Madeline's face lit up when Liberty said the horse was doing much better.

But even after the town veterinarian had left, Madeline stayed, whispering something sweet to Dotty. Then Madeline took her place on the chair again, and Brandon wrapped a blanket around her. After some time, her head drifted to his shoulder, and he was afraid to move and even breathe as tenderness filled his entire being.

Stolen or not, these moments were precious.

Then Ronan showed up with a lunch box. "I won't take credit. Jessie made them, and yes, they are safe to eat." His face lit up as he talked about his wife.

Marriage agreed with Brandon's brother, and Brandon frowned at his twinge of envy. After a painful loss, Ronan hadn't been looking for romance. That was until he met Jessie.

On the contrary, Brandon had wanted a family for a long time, the same everlasting love his parents had. He'd wanted it badly enough he'd almost married his longtime girlfriend, whom he'd cared about but didn't love. That would've been a mistake.

He and Madeline took their chairs outside where stars twinkled in the sky and damp night air met them. He removed his jacket and wrapped it around her shoulders. Normally, she'd protest, but this time she snuggled into it, and he felt as if his soul were wrapped in a jacket, too. While worry for Dotty still nagged at him, the night, so beautiful and romantic, soothed him, creating a forever memory.

Madeline's presence would make any night beautiful and romantic. Even one spent with a sick horse.

While he updated his brother on Dotty's condition, Madeline sank into the chair, her every movement graceful.

Then Ronan handed her one of the sandwiches. "Lean turkey and lettuce on rye bread as Jessie said you preferred." He gave Brandon a sandwich loaded with ham and cheese and pickles between generous slices of Mom's homemade soda bread.

Madeline wrinkled her nose as she stared at her sandwich. "Um. Thank you."

"Would you like to switch?" Brandon offered her his still-wrapped sandwich.

She brightened. "You like rye bread and lettuce?"

Just about as much as she liked carrots.

"It's... it's wonderful." Brandon tried to put some conviction in his words.

Ronan's lips twitched upward. Brandon didn't like rye bread at all, and the family knew it. But for Madeline, he'd eat it and lettuce any time. After Ronan removed chilled bottles of tea from his lunch bag and passed them out, Brandon said grace, and then the food with cold liquid hit the spot.

"Madeline, I hope I won't spoil your appetite if I ask a few questions." Ronan's expression turned serious.

By that time, she'd inhaled most of the sandwich. "Sure. And thank you very much for helping with my case."

"Of course. You're family." Ronan accepted the empty bottle back from her.

Family. Brandon froze. It wasn't like he'd proposed to Madeline. Would he... ever trust she'd say yes enough to try?

Then Ronan added, "You're my sister-in-law. But sadly, I haven't helped you much yet. Jessie and I are going through the list she and Arianna made of your former suitors, and so far, all those people have stayed in Houston. Jessie and

I have been discussing something else. What if the person who assaulted you wasn't connected to your past, but to Brandon's?"

Brandon nearly choked on his *wonderful* sandwich. "What?"

"Sorry, bro." Ronan patted Brandon on the back. "Since Madeline arrived in Cowboy Crossing, you're clearly off the market, which might've upset some of your exes."

Seriously? Brandon coughed again, and Madeline leaned to him, placing a soft warm hand on his shoulder. "Are you okay?"

"I'm... I'm fine." He glared at his brother. "What a preposterous idea."

Rubbing his neck and ducking his head, Ronan shrugged. "We have to look at *all* angles."

"Well, my list of ex-flames doesn't take many pages. It doesn't even take a page." Or half of it, but really, he didn't need to add *that*.

He'd dated in high school and in his twenties. But in his thirties, he'd only had two longtime girlfriends.

"One of my longtime girlfriends left for Florida to be close to her parents. They moved there after retiring." It had hurt then, but he couldn't imagine leaving the ranch. "From what I heard, she's happily married with three children now."

"What about Daphne? You almost married her."

Madeline flinched, and her eyes widened. Was she jealous? He imagined it was always the other way around.

He fidgeted in his chair. His appetite was gone, but he finished his *wonderful* sandpaper-flavored sandwich. After learning how much effort went into raising food, he'd never wasted any.

"Almost married her, huh? You loved her that much," Madeline whispered.

"That's the thing. I realized I didn't love her enough. Not like a man should love his wife. Our relationship was comfortable, and we had a lot in common. She's a cowgirl who loves working at a ranch. She was also everything I'd want in a wife. Or so I thought."

With each word, Madeline's mouth tightened more.

He forced himself to continue. "I thought, with time, I'd grow to love her. I didn't mean to lead her on."

"And yet, you were boyfriend and girlfriend for four years." No accusation hardened Ronan's voice. "You proposed to her. You call that not leading her on?"

Guilt stung, and the sawdust food grated in Brandon's stomach. He looked at the stars as if he could find the answer there. "I proposed because I felt, by that time, I owed it to Daphne to marry her. And fine, I did want a family. Badly. I wanted to have what our parents have. But I couldn't go ahead with our marriage." He cringed thinking of Daphne's tears and screams when he'd told her he was breaking off the engagement. He'd never meant to hurt her.

"Which was two months before Madeline arrived in Cowboy Crossing," Ronan said, not being helpful at all.

Brandon resisted the urge to gnash his teeth. "Exactly. Two months *before*. So Madeline's arrival couldn't have caused the breakup."

"According to my best information source—our mom—Daphne is still not over it. She told her friends you'd get back together, if only Madeline wasn't here." Ronan sent Madeline an apologetic glance.

Brandon groaned, then shifted toward Madeline. "That's not true."

But she shifted away. Then she took off his jacket and handed it back.

Really? She probably had over a hundred exes in her past. He only had two, and she was the one who got upset?

"I'm going to check where Daphne was at the time of the attack," Ronan said.

Brandon moved toward the stable. "And I'm going to check on Dotty."

Great. Just great. He glowered at his brother, acting like the grouch everyone accused him of being since his breakup.

Chapter Seven

HER PHONE RINGING pulled Madeline out of her sleep. Groggily, she reached for her phone on the nightstand. The cobwebs of sleep cleared up at Brandon's name on the screen, and she cuddled back in, cradling the phone in her palm.

After a mostly sleepless night watching Dotty, she'd gone to the lodge at one in the morning. Then she'd slept in. He didn't have the same luxury.

She swiped the screen to accept the call. "Hello, Brandon." She didn't remember anything to compare it to, but his name felt nice on her tongue.

"I wanted to make sure you're okay." Just his voice stirred excitement in her belly.

"I'm fine." Well, as fine as she could be with most of her memory lacking and a possibility of present danger. Knowing he cared this much mattered though, and gratitude settled her excitement. "How is Dotty feeling?"

"Much better today. Thank you for staying yesterday."

"Of course. You're my boyfriend. What's important to you is important to me. Besides, I didn't want Dotty to suffer."

A longing unraveled inside. She didn't just want to hear him. She wanted to see him, to be near him. He obviously wanted to take things slow, and so should she. But that didn't mean they couldn't cook together, for example.

She was out of her element on the ranch, but she was in her element in the kitchen—or so Jessie and Arianna had told her. Madeline wanted to impress Brandon, and she couldn't exactly invite him to observe her doing an autopsy. Not that she could recall how to do it in the first place, and while one could look up cooking videos, she didn't think it was wise to search for instructions online on how to cut dead bodies.

Plus, it wouldn't hurt to do something nice for him, especially after she'd been a bit abrasive after learning about his long-term relationship. She'd had no right to be jealous.

She'd let the pause stretch too much, so she hurried to add, "Would you like to join me for dinner tonight? We could cook together if you'd like."

"I'd love to," he sang out. "What should I bring?"

"Yourself."

That was all she needed from him. To have him by her side. Arianna had mentioned that men had given Madeline diamonds and a multitude of flowers, but Madeline didn't care for any of that now. Was she falling too deep too fast?

After disconnecting, she stumbled into the bathroom. Minutes later, refreshed, she stepped into the hall, and Rusty nearly knocked her over. She leaned over and rubbed his fur. "Good morning. If it's still morning, that is."

He led her to the patio and whined a little.

"I know Jessie let you out. You just want to play, right?" She tilted her head. She shouldn't have shirked her responsibility, but having a good friend in her corner felt good.

Rusty brought the salad-green ball as if to answer yes. She chuckled, picked it up, and opened the patio door, and he bolted outside, scaring some bird into flight. Then he chased a squirrel over the fence.

Watching him play with Brandon in the yard was one of her happy memories after getting hit on the head, tucked inside with care because there were no guarantees in life. That invoked a sigh as well as an appreciation for those happy-moment memories, as few as she had.

She and Rusty played catch for some time, so surely she'd earned something better for breakfast than apple slices.

Then she walked inside and to the kitchen, led by hunger and sizzling bacon. Now that was what she was talking about.

Arianna looked up from the stove. She was dressed in black shorts and another black T-shirt, this one with a zombie on it. They sure had different tastes in clothes. "Care to join me for lunch? Or breakfast in your case?"

"With pleasure. Brandon and I will cook dinner tonight." Madeline refilled Rusty's water bowl and kibble bowl, then washed her hands and started setting the table.

Arianna chuckled. "I have no doubt you'll cook dinner with him *with pleasure*. I'll make myself scarce this evening." She brought eggs from the fridge. "Are you going to make a salad for yourself?"

Riiight. Madeline's empty stomach protested. "Nope. I gave all our carrots to Speckles, and I don't feel like lettuce. What you're having looks great to me."

Arianna chuckled again as she turned on the stove. "Scrambled or sunny-side up?"

"Scrambled, please." Madeline stole a strip of bacon and scooted aside as Arianna swatted at her. "You don't have to leave in the evening just to give me and Brandon privacy."

Despite her lack of memories, their camaraderie came easily now.

Arianna broke eggs in a bowl, added milk, and then whirred the beater. "Don't worry. I need to review the camera recordings from the mansion anyway. Besides, I have a few new translation assignments to get done." She poured the mixture into the skillet.

Madeline placed a slice of bread in a toaster. "Is that what you do for a living? Are you a translator?" No wonder Arianna could easily stay in the lodge and still do her job.

Arianna's hand stilled, and her expression went blank. "Among other things. When in the States, I assist Paisley with her project helping people escape abusive relationships. The rest of the time, I like to travel the world on different assignments."

Madeline expected Arianna to explain what kind of assignments those were, but she didn't elaborate. She clearly didn't like talking about her work. Why such secrecy? But then, Madeline wouldn't share the details of cutting and sawing dead bodies, either. Even if she remembered those details.

Arianna turned off the stove and piled up the food on her plate. "What are you going to cook tonight?"

Huh. And now Arianna was changing the subject. Madeline let her as she got her own food. She opted for orange juice, and Arianna nodded to fill her glass, as well. Then they sat at the round table.

The eggs were nice and fluffy and bacon crunchy, and Madeline had no clue what she was going to make tonight. "I'll have to look up recipes. I'm drawing a blank. Literally."

Arianna sipped her orange juice. "How about tacos? I can email you the recipe. We already have all the ingredients."

Madeline smiled her gratitude. "Thank you." She recalled Arianna's Hispanic heritage. "Is this something your family used to cook?"

Arianna's eyes darkened. "Yes."

Right. Family. That was another thing Arianna didn't talk about. Madeline had better drop that line of conversation.

Something lurked in the shadows of her memory, tinted red, having a strange metallic scent, but she couldn't reach for it. "It's difficult... not to remember." She resolved to go through her phone again and social media to reconstruct pieces of her former life. If she hadn't spent so much time with Brandon, she'd have done it already. But no matter how much time she spent with him, she craved his presence.

How was it possible to miss him this much if she'd just seen him yesterday? Today even, considering she'd returned home around one in the morning.

Arianna clattered the fork back on her plate. "You will remember everything. One day." She said it in a strange tone as if she weren't sure it would be a good thing. "Until then, we'll be your memory. I'll fill you in on some things."

"Thanks." It wasn't the same, but it was something. "It'll be like watching a movie of my life you've recorded in your mind." Madeline munched on crunchy bacon. The smell she recognized, but the taste was weirdly unfamiliar. But it didn't make it any less yummy.

Maybe she should've agreed to some of the therapy the hospital physician suggested. But it meant regular trips to Springfield, and she'd much rather spend time with Brandon and her foster sisters. Besides, even the word *therapy* gave her an uneasy feeling in her stomach.

Arianna resumed eating. She ate fast as if she were used to hurrying instead of savoring food. And just as fast, she filled Madeline in on the last decade of her life. Then she said, "By the way, we're meeting Jessie for coffee in Springfield in two hours. She'll answer your questions about your childhood better. I joined you all when you were already a teenager. Besides, as you can see, I'm not like these eggs. I'm not warm and fluffy. I don't do relationships well."

"Why do I have a feeling the same can be said about me?" On her part, Madeline savored every bite of her breakfast, but the thought of them both not doing relationships well still unsettled her. "But I'd never guess that about you. You've been wonderful to me."

Arianna's eyes softened. "You and the girls are my exceptions."

Huh. Yet she didn't share about her work or her family. Obviously, despite making her foster sisters an exception to the rule, she didn't let even them get close.

Madeline studied her foster sister over the rim of her glass. "We both keep people at arm's length, don't we?"

Arianna drained her glass, her green eyes once again unreadable. "That we do."

By the evening, Madeline changed outfits several times before settling on a long summer dress with a sweetheart neckline and short sleeves. The color matched her eyes, and the smooth fabric shimmered around her legs.

Not exactly an appropriate outfit for cooking, especially considering food splatter could ruin the dress, but she'd already learned that she'd rarely followed conventions.

Her heart skipped a beat as she wanted to see Brandon's reaction to her dress, and she wasn't disappointed. His eyebrows shot up when he stepped inside the lodge.

She was used to seeing him in worn-out jeans and Wrangler's shirts. But these jeans looked brand new, and the ice-blue button-down shirt looked ironed. He handed her a bouquet of pink roses. "Did I mix up something? Are we staying in to cook, or are we going out to eat at some fancy place?"

She breathed in the beautiful aroma. Maybe she'd been wrong before because a pleasant wave spread inside her. She liked receiving flowers when they came from him. "Staying in. And thank you for the roses."

Then she zeroed in on the second object in his hands—a fishbowl. Instead of water and fish, it contained folded magenta, yellow, and green Post-its. "Um, what is this?" She gestured for him to follow her into the kitchen where she filled a vase with water and placed the flowers on the knotty pine table.

He shifted from one foot to the other, then slid the fishbowl close to the flowers. "I don't know if it was a good idea. But it's sort of a memory jar."

"A memory jar?"

Rubbing the back of his neck, he studied the floor. "A memory fishbowl in this case. I wrote some of the good memories I have about you on Post-its. I left a few blank. I thought maybe your foster sisters could fill the rest. Was it a bad idea?"

Her heart swelling, she threw her arms around his neck. "It was a great idea. That was very thoughtful."

His face lit up, and he stared into her eyes as his arms encircled her waist. Pleasant tingles erupted over her skin. Awareness filled her, and she allowed herself a few blissful moments in his arms.

Something about his words bothered her, though. What was it? He said "some of the good memories." Did that mean there were a lot of not-good memories?

She did her best to keep the thought from spoiling her joy from the gift. Every relationship has its issues. Though...

Arianna's words earlier made Madeline wonder...

If Madeline didn't let people close, did that include Brandon?

She eased out of his embrace. Until she could figure out her own mind and memories, she'd best be careful. Or maybe some inner resistance warred with her attraction. She might not know much about herself, but she sensed trust didn't come easy.

His eyes dulled, but he didn't say anything.

Her stomach tightened. He kept doing nice things for her, and she kept messing up.

She did her best to concentrate on the positive. "I can't wait to read what you wrote, but we should start on the food."

"Seeing you happy is more important to me than food." He sounded so sincere. Surely, she could trust him. So what erected that inner barrier?

Not the attraction because that was flaring up hot inside her. She longed to kiss him on the lips, but she settled on pressing her lips to his slightly rough cheek. "Okay."

She reached into the bowl and took out a salad-green Post-it Note. Then she unfolded it. His handwriting was easy to read, letters large and solid like the man himself.

"The first time I saw you, you wore a long cream-colored knit dress and were sitting on the sofa covered with a navy blanket. Your hand was in a cast, and a bruise mottled the side of your face." She stopped as Brandon ran out of space. Probably not the best memory she wanted to have of herself. But he did remember the first time he'd met her, and that was something.

"I stuck another Post-it to this one," he said softly. "There wasn't enough space."

Her breath caught in her throat as she kept reading. "But I'd never seen anyone so beautiful. You were like a morning star. I knew that, from then on, you wouldn't be just the brightest star for me. You'd be the only one."

"Wow. That was amazing." Her heart shifted. "Did I have the same reaction to you?"

He frowned. "I don't think so. But you were cranky after the accident."

In other words, she hadn't treated him well in the beginning. Surely, that had changed with time.

Now she needed to start cooking before she began sniffling. Yet she read another. That was about the first time she'd smiled at him and how it had brightened his world.

As much as she wanted to keep reading, she stopped herself. "This means a lot to me."

"And *you* mean a lot to me." He stopped as if uncomfortable over having said so much.

She wanted to say the same back to him, but she struggled with the words. So she turned to a safer topic. "I already defrosted the meat. Would you like to simmer it in the skillet while I cut vegetables?"

Again, the light in his eyes dimmed.

Argh.

She'd been the one to want him to be more affectionate with her, and now when he was, at least with his words, she was pulling back. Why? Only to assert the independence that had been slipping these last days? Or was there more to it? The attachment issue Arianna had told her all their foster sisters had? Childhood trauma? Everything combined?

How could she figure out their relationship and the world around her when she couldn't even figure out herself?

She touched his forearm. "I–I don't know how to express what I feel. Or what I am supposed to feel. Or what I'm supposed to know. It's all... confusing. But I'll get there eventually."

This time, the sadness in his eyes made her ache. "Will you, though? Or can simple cowboys like me only dream about stars like you?"

What? Even having nothing to compare him with, she could see what a catch he was. And she felt far from being a star. Currently, she didn't even have a job. Or a house of her own because the lodge didn't belong to her, but to her foster sister who was now in Germany. Or any recollections.

Her life was a mess, and he was the only certain thing in it, her anchor in a storm. "Of course, I will. Just... be patient with me."

He nodded but looked unconvinced. Then he strode to the sink and washed his hands. "I've got the meat part."

You mean a lot to me, too.

Why was it so difficult to say those simple words?

She took lettuce and tomatoes out of the fridge and started slicing lettuce. Her hands flew as if regaining muscle memory. She was good with the knife indeed.

He turned on the stove and poured oil into the skillet. "This is not on any Post-it. I caught you looking out the window once. I've never seen eyes more beautiful—or more forlorn. I ached to see your eyes laugh. That evening, I suggested watching romantic comedies. After the second one, I finally heard your laugh. But there was still some sadness in your eyes."

Her hand with the knife froze in the air.

He was making himself vulnerable to her, and he was giving part of her back to her. She gave him a grateful smile. But now when she knew more about herself, she couldn't do the same in return. She didn't want to be vulnerable more than the loss of memory and current threat of danger had made her.

Would she ever?

She looked up at his broad chest, then the muscles he'd earned not in the gym but by hard work outdoors. It drove back the point about being her anchor in the storm, but also made appreciation simmer under her skin like the food simmered in the skillet.

"If you want to know more about yourself, feel free to ask." He crumbled the meat into the skillet.

Could she do it? Ask those get-to-know-you questions—about herself? It felt like a weird game. Like getting to know a stranger. A stranger who was herself. She looked up from the cutting board. "What's my favorite flower?" He'd brought roses. "Never mind. Roses." She wasn't very original there, was she?

She thought a moment. "What about my favorite color?" Would he know?

He didn't hesitate. "Turquoise. The color of the sky on a sunny day. Other shades of blue, as well."

She did see a lot of shades of blue in her closet. Would she paint the lodge walls blue if she owned it? Her heart squeezed a little. It was a temporary home, and one more reason she felt suspended in time. No job, no house, no parents, no relatives who cared about her.

Arianna had told her about a large Houston home with expensive furnishings that Madeline had sold after her divorce. Cold traveled down her spine. After what had happened there, no wonder she hadn't wanted to stay.

Her heart shifted painfully. But she had Brandon and her foster sisters. She'd spent a lot of time with Arianna and Jessie, who'd been giving her back pieces of herself. She'd video conferenced with Genevieve, who'd stayed in Houston because her daughter had been sick, and Paisley who was in Germany.

While she'd been trying to get to know her foster sisters almost as much as she'd tried to get to know herself, she could see what a treasure they were, what an incredible bond they shared.

Hmm. While trying to learn more about herself, she'd forgotten to learn about Brandon. He seemed open, everything on the surface, and she was grateful. It was enough having so many mysteries lurking in her past already.

"What's *your* favorite color?" she asked.

"Also blue. Because it's the color of your eyes." His face pinked a little above his beard as he added spices to the meat. The spice aromas spread in the air. "I found a new world in your eyes."

She found a new world in his eyes, too.

The words and his embarrassment endeared him to her even more. From anyone else, those words might've sounded cheesy. From him, they sounded sincere. She couldn't believe both Arianna and Jessie had said Brandon was a grouch. He was different with her.

Or was it because he pitied her for her memory loss? He loved helping people and animals. Could it be that he'd been drawn to her simply because she needed help?

The thought didn't sit well with her. More reason to try to assert her independence. She wanted to be liked, but she didn't want to be seen as weak.

Her questions lacked depth, and maybe it wasn't a good sign. She didn't ask what her favorite car was. That much was obvious, based on the red Ferrari in the garage. She liked expensive, flashy things. Did she lack depth, too? Or was the showiness expected of her, based on her looks? Or both?

Her gaze shifted to a peach cobbler his mother had baked for her homecoming, and an image flashed in her mind. She'd seen a snippet of a peach cobbler in her mind before, but it had disappeared too fast.

The scent of a freshly baked dessert floated from the memory, and her stealing a tiny piece that melted in her mouth. A sunlit kitchen, smaller than this one and filled with knickknacks and bright towels with pictures of peaches and apples. A woman's laughter.

Mom.

Madeline had recognized the voice before she recognized the face.

"Be patient. Dinner before dessert," the voice was melodic, cheerful. "Let's go to the garden and cut some roses to make the table look pretty. Daddy will like it."

Madeline had giggled then but with a tinge of nervousness. They'd both wanted to make him happy. Another scent floated, this time of roses and grass....

Later, she'd sneaked into the garden and cut three more pink roses, not paying attention to the thorns scratching her hand. Inside the house, she'd poured water into a heavy crystal vase, and her muscles strained as she'd carried it and the roses in it to his office. She wasn't usually allowed there, but she'd wanted to make it look pretty, surprise him. But when she'd put the vase on the table, it had slipped and knocked down a porcelain fisherman figurine.

Terrified, she'd watched it land on the hardwood floor.

"Daddy's home!" Her mother's singsong voice had made Madeline tremble.

Maybe she could glue the porcelain together. She crouched near the shards.

The door opened. His face grew hard, and his eyes narrowed. "You broke it."

"I'm so sorry, Daddy," she whispered.

"Leave the room."

"Daddy, please!" She begged as she walked past him, her head low.

He stepped inside. "You're such a disappointment."

The door slammed in her face, and Madeline started bawling. All she'd ever wanted was for Daddy to love her, to be proud of her. In so many senses, she'd looked up to the man everyone had said was a brilliant surgeon. But even at six, she'd already understood that some things, once broken, couldn't be glued together....

Distracted, she stopped paying attention to the vegetables, then flinched at a sharp pain.

She stared at the drop of blood on her finger. Something edged at the corners of her memory again, and she shuddered. She'd seen blood before. Lots of it.

Against white sheets...

Her fingers tightened. She'd carried something with her then. A doll? How old was she? Seven? A small child still. Terror grasped her heart. A scent permeated everything then. A metallic scent... Her father's lips moving, but she couldn't hear the words. The smooth phone dropping from her hands, covered in sticky liquid... Then a different scent. Foliage and grass.

Her father was right to call her a disappointment. If only she'd woken up that night. If only she'd heard the intruder. If only she'd been able to stop him from bleeding out instead of running outside.

Brandon turned around, and his brow furrowed. "Are you okay?"

She couldn't form a word, so she just shook her head.

"You cut yourself. I'll get the first aid kit." He disappeared in the direction of the bathroom.

She wanted to say she was going to get it, but he knew the lodge and everything in it better than she did. He knew her better than she did.

Red... So much red... Soaked in red... The doll hitting the floor.

He was back before the memory could encroach on her again. He led her to the sink and let water wash over the cut. If only she could wash away the memory as easily! Why couldn't she have remembered something nice and pleasant, like their first kiss?

Strangely enough, her memories didn't take her to recent events, but to decades ago. Not to the things she wanted to remember, but to the things she didn't.

He turned off the stove and treated the cut with an antibiotic cream. "Thankfully, it doesn't look too deep."

Yes, her other wounds ran way deeper. She knew it now. And she didn't mean those cuts on her stomach she'd apparently inflicted on herself in her teens, though they were bothersome, too.

He wrapped a Band-Aid in place and searched her eyes. "There's something else, isn't there?"

She nodded. Her tongue felt swollen and foreign. "A ghost of a memory. It must be from when I found my parents. But it was still... fuzzy."

Guilt slammed into her, and she nearly staggered. Yes, she'd only been seven, but her father was still alive when she'd found him. If she'd stayed to help instead of running outside, terrified... Her mistake had cost him his life, and consequently, the lives of all the people he could've saved.

"I'm sorry that's the one memory that came back to you." He hugged her and kept her close. "I'll keep praying for you."

Then he rocked her a little, and for several moments, everything was almost all right with her world because he was in it.

Chapter Eight

NERVES GOT THE BETTER of Brandon. He was usually a confident man, and whenever he was out of his element, like he'd been with Madeline before she got amnesia, he'd covered it with grouchiness.

However, treating Madeline badly when she needed him would make him a jerk, and that he wasn't. He should walk away from her now before she walked away from him, but he felt a nudge to stay by her side. Was it God's will? Or was it Brandon's thinking?

Besides giving her literature and movies, he'd talked to her about Jesus, and she'd asked questions. To most of them, he'd had answers, but to her main one—why God allowed so much suffering in the world, like letting her parents die—Brandon hadn't. How could he bring her closer to God if he couldn't persuade her God was merciful?

Lord, please guide me.

There was another reason for his nerves today, too. Visiting an art gallery in Springfield shouldn't be a big deal. If not for a small secret only his family knew about.

How would Madeline react?

He stole a glance at her as they passed the town limits in his rusty truck, such a contrast to the red Ferrari she cruised through town in. Her profile was beautiful, and her luscious chestnut-hued hair flowing over her shoulders would make a shampoo producer proud.

He inhaled her faint lavender scent and kept it in for a few seconds, wishing he could keep her in, as well. Then the air rushed from his lungs as a thought sucker punched him. He had to tell her about their breakup. He'd kept it from her for too long already. The fact that she'd started remembering some things from her past spurred him on.

But if he did, she'd leave him, and then he wouldn't be able to help her while her life was in danger. Matt Luettgen was still on the loose, and the identity of her attacker was unknown. As she started to recall the tragic deaths of her parents, there could be a chance she'd remember some important detail before the assault that could've put the culprit at risk of being discovered after all these years. Probably unlikely, but possible.

Brandon didn't believe his former girlfriend might've wanted to harm his new one, even if she'd said she'd been alone at that time and, therefore, didn't have an alibi.

Madeline was in danger, and she needed him to protect her. She needed him to comfort her as her world was still confusing and the first memories that floated into her mind were mostly painful.

Or was that an excuse he kept telling himself? His life had been straightforward so far, and he was a straightforward guy. So keeping this important detail from her gnawed at him.

Lord, please forgive me.

Most likely, Madeline never would once she found out. His second chance with her wasn't much of an opportunity, and he wouldn't get a third.

"You don't have to go to the art gallery just because you think I'd like it." Her melodic voice interrupted his musings.

"I want to. Believe me." A drop of sweat trickled down his back. Just great. His deodorant better hold up.

"Then I appreciate it." She touched his arm, her hand warm.

Just that simple gesture sent a punch to his heart, and his heart was shaky today to start with.

It wasn't like it was a big secret, really. His family knew. But how would she react? Her taste was the best of the best. He was proud of his origins and honored to work on the family ranch. But with her, he sometimes felt like a stable boy with a princess.

He'd made the mistake of helping Ronan go over the list of her suitors. The level of those men had made Brandon grind his molars. Celebrities and executives who could give her diamonds and cars and anything else she wanted. He'd sent a friend request on social media when they'd started dating so they could communicate online, as well. Not his brightest idea, especially after he'd seen a famous singer dedicating a song to her. Not to mention the kinds of events she'd attended.

One of the photos some time after her divorce showed the flowers she'd received. Rose bouquets in fancy vases covered her entire living room floor. A sea of roses. Hundreds, maybe even thousands of them. The small bouquet of three roses he'd brought yesterday looked pitiful in comparison. She was destined to live in a palace and shine at the best events with senators and celebrities. Once she regained her memory, she'd realize it.

What could Brandon, a simple cowboy, do for her, really?

She'd dated the cream of society, and he was… the bread, and not exactly a fancy kind.

He switched the radio station from country to classical. "You like classical music."

She switched it back. "I'd better warn you—I don't always have to stick to the same things I'd once liked. I hope you can forgive me for a few changes because country sounds good right now."

Hmm. It wasn't like she'd needed to maintain an image here. Putting on a shirt without stains was dressing up for him, or at least it had been before she'd shown up. She hadn't always maintained an image in Houston—after all, she must've worn scrubs to work. So why did she have to always be so perfect, so elegant, so unreachable when she'd arrived in their small town?

Many people still gossiped about her gowns and shoes.

Belatedly, he checked for a tail the way his cop brother had taught him to. He should've done that already. Argh. With several cars behind him, who could say whether any had followed them from Cowboy Crossing? Was he kidding himself to think he could be her bodyguard?

He carried his firearm with him now, and like all his brothers, he knew how to use it. But he didn't have the other necessary skills for a bodyguard.

He told Madeline as much.

She shook her head, sending that gorgeous hair flying. "You're my boyfriend, *not* my bodyguard. You're here with me. That's all that matters to me."

He put his arm on the console, and she laced her fingers through his, sending a pleasant jolt through him. But at the same time, guilt knifed him. If he hadn't pretended to be her boyfriend, if she hadn't lost her memory, she wouldn't be placing her hand in his now.

He should tell her.

Now. Swallowing hard, he eased up on the gas, took a deep breath of the lavender scent that drove him crazy, and started, "I wanted to—"

Her phone rang, and she sent him an apologetic glance. "Sorry. It's Jessie. I've got to take this. Might be an update on Matt Luettgen's whereabouts."

"Of course." He shouldn't be glad about the delay.

But he was. He was falling for her all over again while keeping her nearby on false pretenses.

After talking for some time, she slid her phone into her elegant purse. He glanced at her before returning his attention to the road. Her eyes narrowed. Tension curdled in the air like sour milk.

"Is everything okay?" he asked.

"Matt Luettgen's uncle's car was found near Springfield."

That's too close for comfort.

Alarm sliced through him, and his fingers tightened around the steering wheel. The danger was real. He couldn't tell her about their breakup until he knew she was safe or at least until they found Luettgen. Brandon might not have great bodyguard skills, but he'd give up his life for her.

Neither of them said a word.

Did it bother her that he wasn't much of a conversationalist? He'd never known how to talk to the ladies and often covered awkwardness with grouchiness. It was one of the many reasons he preferred working with horses and cows to talking to people.

He'd done the same with Madeline at first, especially considering their differences. Then he'd realized she didn't need him to talk much. Before their breakup, they could be sitting on the sofa watching a romantic comedy or walking in the forest, her hand in his, without saying a word. She wasn't much of a talker, either, and she'd seemed to like their companionable silence. Just her presence had filled a void in him then. And surprisingly, his presence had seemed to do the same for her.

He passed a gray sedan and glanced in the rearview mirror again. Was there a tail or not?

"It's going to be all right." He grumbled it, though he'd wanted to sound kind.

"Of course, it will be." Her voice was unusually soft. "Because you're with me."

Her trust sent both a jolt of shame and a jolt of gratitude through him. He stole a glance at her and caught her smiling back.

His grip on the steering wheel relaxed. He needed to trust that God had a plan for this. That it was going to work out for the better somehow.

Everything about Madeline, from her voice to her smile, was softer now, more open, and strangely even more relaxed despite the danger. Her words and her attitude used to be as sharp as the scalpel she'd once worked with, but not any longer.

Was this the real Madeline before she'd learned to put up defenses after so many horrible things had happened to her? The way she could be if she'd grown up in a caring family like he had without witnessing the gruesome effects of murder on the people dearest to her?

He hadn't realized it at first, but while he'd always admired the way she looked, he'd maybe looked down on her a little because of what he'd considered her superficial moral qualities. Some people in Cowboy Crossing had considered her stuck-up and, yes, a tad snobbish.

He was a Christian and had done his best to help others and work hard. She'd seemed to be all about appearances and flashy outfits and appeared to go through life without caring about other people's feelings, including his.

What he hadn't thought of was that maybe all that was a defense mechanism she employed to prevent herself from being hurt again. Now, who was the superficial and snobbish one? Not to mention, he wasn't as honest as he'd considered himself to be. He hadn't told her about their breakup yet, even if for noble reasons.

Once at the gallery, he tensed. The place smelled faintly of oil paints and perfumes. In an elegant turquoise dress that swirled to her ankles, she looked way more suited to the place than he did, even if he wore a buttoned-down shirt he'd bought for the occasion. She was born to be admired, confirmed by people's looks everywhere they'd gone.

The beautiful place with exquisite paintings suited her. She was a work of art—no, more than that, a masterpiece. And he was, what, a paintbrush, maybe?

He had another reason for his apprehension. She'd come from a city famous for art galleries, among other things. And this wasn't a grand opening with people in suits and evening gowns carrying flutes of champagne.

Would this modest exhibition of landscapes and still lifes impress her? His heart skipped a beat. Even more importantly for him, would what awaited them in the next room impress her?

Her blue eyes sparkled as she turned to him. "I love this. Thank you for bringing me here."

"I had a bit of a selfish reason to bring you here. I have something to show you." He might as well tell her. She was going to see the signature anyway.

"Ooooh. I'm intrigued."

His heart beating fast, he led her to the next room.

She moved slowly along a large painting of the lake at sunrise, then stepped to the next one. He held his breath. The scenery of an emerald-hued field with its bright-blue cloudless sky and a palomino mare with its foal probably paled in comparison to the gorgeous colors of the sunrise. It was simple. No fancy techniques or hidden meanings.

She stayed awhile near the western landscape. Would she guess it? "It's beautiful. Everything about it. The nature. The mother's love. The adorable little one."

He perked up. "We just had a foal at the ranch. Though there's not much mother's love there. The mare rejected her."

Her face brightened. "Can I see the foal? Please?"

"Sure. I'll call you tomorrow, and you can come feed her."

"Oooh." Her megawatt smile was magazine-cover worthy. "Thanks." Then she zoomed in on the signature, and her eyebrows shot up. "Is this a namesake or... This is yours, isn't it?"

He nodded, searching her eyes for her reaction. "I didn't go to art school. I just paint what I see."

"Then it's even more incredible." Her eyes widened. "I didn't realize you're this talented."

Finally, he drew a breath. "Do you mean it?"

"Of course! Congratulations!" She threw her arms around him and hugged him, then let him go too soon. Then understanding apparently dawned on her. "The landscape paintings at your parents' house... They are yours, aren't they?"

Again, he nodded.

Her eyes lit up, and she clapped. "We need to organize a personal exhibition for you."

Though flattered, he felt like choking. One painting out was okay, but to stuff himself in a suit and have people judge and discuss his work... "I don't have enough paintings." Unless one counted all the portraits of her he'd painted, but she didn't need to know that. "And I'm a cowboy first and an artist second."

Her blue eyes turned pensive. "I complained about people stereotyping me because of my appearance. But I guess I stereotyped you, too. There's so much more to you than I realized." She turned around and stared at the painting again.

Would she see his love for the place that had made him the man he was?

He didn't want fancy exhibitions with fancy openings. Even the buttoned-down shirt suffocated him. He definitely didn't want to don a tie and tux, didn't want to mingle with arty types who knew way more than he did about culture. But she'd fit perfectly at such an event.

His heart shifted. A rare beauty like her belonged in a stunning evening gown at a gala, not in scuffed cowboy boots in an open field. Was he trying to put a diamond in a steel ring instead of a golden setting? He'd found the place he loved without searching for it, by simply being born into it. She also deserved to be in a place that made her happy, a place where she could shine.

He couldn't be a cloud hiding the bright star that she was from the world. The right thing would be to let her go when the time came and to prepare himself for it.

No matter how heartbreaking.

Chapter Nine

A DAY LATER, Brandon joined Kieran in the stable as his brother bottle-fed their newest addition, a tiny bay foal with a half-moon on its forehead.

Brandon may have been the oldest in the family, but Kieran, the fourth in their lineup, sure acted like the typical eldest brother, wiser and more responsible than his siblings. Often, Brandon felt the closest to Kieran because they shared their dedication to the ranch and ranch animals and their responsibility for it. Kieran also nursed a broken heart. The woman he'd fallen in love with didn't enjoy ranch life and left for big city lights—and a more polished man.

While mares rarely rejected their foals, humans left other humans all the time.

Brandon's heart squeezed from compassion for the rejected foal and for his rejected—in a different way—brother. But would Madeline leave Brandon in a similar way? She didn't fit on the ranch any more than Kieran's ex had. Besides, she had no chance to work as a medical examiner here. Brandon wouldn't blame her if she left.

Still, his gut twisted, and his nerves strained. But like always, he let the animals soothe him. He crouched near the adorable foal, tenderness filling him. Thankfully, they already had colostrum, or mare milk, stored and available to provide. "Her mother still wouldn't nurse her?"

"Nope." Kieran shook his head. "I tried to distract her with feed. Smeared the little one with her mother's sweat and milk."

Liberty had already checked the horse to make sure her udder wasn't swollen and ensure she wasn't experiencing any other discomfort that would cause her to refuse to nurse. At least, she wasn't aggressive and didn't bite the foal.

Although, as the oldest, Brandon was supposed to take over managing the ranch from their father, Kieran worked right alongside him on that and did the rest of the paperwork Brandon just couldn't handle. Brandon felt more comfortable in the open field than crouching behind the desk in a small office, trying to make sense of numbers. Kieran could've passed the bottle-feeding duty to someone else, but Brandon suspected his brother enjoyed it.

He had a selfish reason for joining Kieran besides watching the sweet scene. "I need advice."

Kieran nodded as he moved the bottle slightly to give the foal better access to the colostrum. He didn't look surprised in the least. Everyone in the family turned to him for advice, including their extended family of ranch hands and their friends and neighbors. If horses could talk, they'd ask him for advice, as well.

So Kieran already knew about the situation with Madeline.

"I can't walk away from her if she needs my protection. But once I tell her we'd broken up or she remembers it, she'll be the one walking away."

"And she matters to you very much." Kieran frowned. Was he recalling his similar situation that ended in a disaster? He'd chosen the ranch over love then. Had he ever regretted it? Then he ironed out his frown as he patted the foal.

Brandon crouched near the little one. "Despite our differences and the fact she might be leaving soon and…. Yes, she does matter to me very much."

Kieran's lips flattened, and his gaze turned pensive. "Then I see only one way out. You need her to fall in love with you before she remembers the breakup or you tell her about it."

That sounded easier said than done. "How do I do that?"

"Just be yourself." Kieran removed the empty bottle.

Brandon snorted. "I *was* myself, and she broke up with me. Remember?"

"Maybe it wasn't *you* she broke up with, but her own fear. That can only change once you become more important to her than what's holding her back."

That didn't sound much easier. Brandon prayed for God's help, then prayed for the rejected foal and for the future foals. She was their first one this spring, arriving earlier than expected, and the first foal being rejected by the mare wasn't a good sign.

Then a rare smile crinkled up Kieran's cheeks. "You have a secret weapon right here. Bring Madeline to feed this foal."

"I already promised her that."

"Good." Kieran nodded as he patted the foal with tenderness. "Ask her to name the little one. How can Madeline not fall in love with this cutie?"

The foal stepped forward on long wobbly legs as if to second that question.

Brandon was asking himself a similar question. How could he not fall in love with Madeline?

Madeline couldn't wait to go meet the foal. And okay, fine, she couldn't wait to see Brandon. The more she learned about him, the more drawn to him she felt.

Something was incredibly touching about a broad-shouldered, strong man feeding a little foal from a bottle with gentleness and care. The contrast of that gentleness to his strength wasn't lost on her.

Tenderness expanded her heart as she shamelessly watched him. Yesterday, she'd flipped through glossy magazines with glammed-up images of herself in her model years. Some of them were with dashing male models. But none of those handsome men compared to the one in front of her. None made her heart race like he did.

If the scene hadn't been so intimate, it should be in a commercial because she'd be buying whatever he was selling.

And the little one just stole her heart the moment Madeline saw her. "May I try it?" She gestured to the bottle.

His smile was soft. "Of course."

Their hands touched when he handed her the bottle, and pleasant tingles cascaded over her skin. Did she always have this strong reaction to him? Well, duh, there was a reason he was her boyfriend. But why hadn't he kissed her yet? Was her attraction to him way bigger than his attraction to her? Why oh why couldn't she remember?

But she couldn't be mistaken about the way his breathing quickened or his eyes darkened. He *was* attracted to her, and that gave her a jolt of satisfaction. Awareness swirled in the air filled with the scents of hay and horses.

The foal let the bottle slip and neighed pitifully.

"Oh, sorry." Madeline broke eye contact with Brandon and placed the bottle's tip in the foal's mouth. The little one latched onto it, emptying it fast.

It made Madeline laugh. "What's her name?"

"We didn't name her yet. How about you do it?"

"Really?" She would've clapped if her hands weren't occupied with the bottle.

"Really." His eyes were kind.

"Okay." She felt giddy like a child at a county fair. County fair... The aroma of popcorn... The taste of cotton candy... The sound of music... Something moving... A carousel? She'd been holding onto her parents' hands, but then they'd let her go when buying more cotton candy. She'd stumbled and fallen. Her knee had been busted, blood gushing.

Her father's voice was soothing. "It's okay. I'll clean it up and bandage it. It's going to be as good as new."

He did care about her! If she was hurt, if she cut herself, he'd comfort her. Even if she was a disappointment to him.

The image and the scents and the sweetness she nearly felt on her tongue poked at her memories but didn't stay. Maybe one day they would. Or was she creating her memories right now, like a movie on demand?

Once she finished the feeding, Brandon and Madeline moved on to grooming the horses.

"I need to tell you something." His shoulders rolled with tension.

That tension rolled inside her, too. Based on that and the tightness of his jaw, she wasn't going to like it. Premonition flushed over her like a dirty puddle splashed by a passing car if she didn't jump back fast enough.

She did want to jump back. It was the second time he tried to tell her something, and based on his frown and the tension in the air she didn't want to hear it. Their relationship was too precious for them to stir up muddy waters. She had enough of those in her mind, obscuring her past.

Kieran entered the stable. "Hello, Madeline. Hey, bro. There you are. Mom is asking whether you both would like to join us for dinner."

She released a breath, grateful for the interruption and the tension slipping from Brandon's jaw. "I'd love to. I can help cook." She had a selfish reason to volunteer. She loved spending time with Brandon's mother.

Had she cooked with her own? That peach cobbler had been home-baked. The scents of meatloaf and fried russet potatoes floated from far corners of her memory. That sunlit kitchen with knickknacks and cheery towels looked well-loved. Was Madeline well-loved? She had to believe she was. The family photos she treasured and displayed in the lodge showed a beautiful, smiling family. Even if her father's smile had started to look a bit strained over time and a trace of guilt tainted her mother's. Or maybe Madeline was reading too much into it.

She might have a lot of gaps in her knowledge about herself, but she knew where she'd come from, was proud of it, needed that badly.

Brandon simply nodded.

She didn't have a good idea of how a family should be, but she had a strong feeling the O'Neills were an example of that. Her own family must've been, too. When it had existed. She did her best to ignore a painful pang at the thought.

"Great. I'll let Mom know." Kieran looked from Madeline to his brother and back, and a satisfied smile crinkled up his tanned face. Just why did he look like a cat who'd eaten the canary?

"Thank you for the invite." She mulled over what she knew about Kieran.

Responsible, hardworking, and a silent type who got things done without bragging. He seemed to be a good influence on his siblings and the people around him. He'd lived at the ranch his entire life and now helped manage it. She watched him check on the horses and marked his affection for animals as a huge plus. What a shame a great guy like him was single.

Just like it was a shame Arianna was single. The more Madeline knew her foster sister, the more she wanted her to find someone who'd make her feel the way Brandon made Madeline feel. Though, of course, that would be a tall order. She sent him an affectionate gaze as he helped his brother.

Kieran had a commanding presence—calm, solid, and stable, firmly settled in one place, and exactly the opposite of Arianna, who seemed listless and nomadic, searching for something even she probably didn't know herself.

But could Kieran be what Arianna needed? Or would this end in disaster? Madeline didn't know what kind of deep soul wound prevented Arianna from finding a significant other. Madeline's instincts told her it wasn't because she didn't remember it, but because Arianna never shared it with anyone. Considering the bond between foster sisters, that was surprising, even alarming.

Kieran and Arianna must've already met at Jessie's wedding or Paisley's wedding. If only Madeline could search her memory for any sparks between them! But as things were, she only had one way to find out.

Likely she'd never been a matchmaker, and she'd best not start now. Yet she had a nudge to ask, "Would it be okay if I ask Arianna to join us for dinner?"

The way Kieran's eyes lit up spoke volumes. "Sure." There were sparks on his side.

He left, and Madeline called her foster sister. At Brandon's suggestion, she also invited Genevieve and Gold since they'd arrived this morning, after Gold recovered from her tummy bug.

Then Madeline started brushing Speckles's mane while Brandon placed the feed. She was getting attached to this gorgeous horse already, and the brushstrokes calmed some disquiet in her heart. Could she see a future for herself here? Or did that disquiet and restlessness mean she needed to reexplore life in the big city? Was she happy there?

She wasn't born a cowgirl, and even the word felt strange like someone else's dress that was too big and threatened to slip off and expose her true self.

But each stroke and Brandon's quiet presence brought a sense of peace she craved. Almost as much as she craved his company. Wasn't that the point, though? She needed first to reconnect with the outside world to know what she was missing.

It was unfair to her and, for that matter, to him to have her world revolve around him. She patted the beautiful Appaloosa's smooth coat. Brandon handed her a carrot, and she made a mental note to bring some next time. She gave it to the horse and felt a tickle on her palm as the Appaloosa lipped the carrot.

She laughed. "Brandon, I can see why you love working at the ranch."

"It's hard but rewarding work." Joy in his job warmed his voice.

He'd found his place in life, but she hadn't. Not because of memory loss. Based on what she'd learned from Arianna, Madeline had floundered after quitting her job and terminating the rent on her Houston apartment.

He had a purpose in life, even several. Her father had saved lives, and so did Paisley by helping abused people escape and then change their lives. Arianna assisted in that project, plus those mysterious assignments must've served a purpose, as well. Genevieve taught eager young minds and raised a daughter on her own. Ronan and Jessie protected people, often saving lives, too.

But what was Madeline's purpose in life now?

Another memory surfaced. A voice. An angry voice. Male. A scent of expensive cologne. Could she hear the words? Yes.

"I expected you to quit your job after marrying me. Don't you have a large house with expensive things already? I don't limit you in expenses for your wardrobe. My wife should look good."

Her own voice, tired. "I love my job. I'm good at it."

"I don't want you to wear scrubs and smell like dead people. Telling people about your job embarrasses me. I have high aspirations you knew about, and I expect you to do your part." A pause when she didn't say anything. "You're such a disappointment as a wife."

There it was again, that word that cut razor-sharp. *Disappointment.*

Really?

These were the things she remembered? Why couldn't she have happy memories back instead?

Based on the words, the voice belonged to her husband. She didn't fit his world the way he'd wanted her to. Maybe she'd tried, as depicted in the many photos she'd found of herself attending different functions with him, wearing a bright smile and a stunning gown. Even after his betrayal, she'd kept those photos. But she'd drawn the line at quitting her job. Which she *had* quit anyway in the end.

Was that the reason she'd kept many people at a distance? If they didn't know her well, they'd only see a beautiful image.

Would she be a disappointment for Brandon one day? A city girl who knew nothing about ranching didn't fit his world, either.

Brushing her fingers over Speckles's smooth coat soothed her nerves a bit.

As Speckles looked at her with large soulful eyes, Madeline was reluctant to move to another horse, so she started braiding the mare's magnificent mane.

Strangely enough, curiosity about Brandon needled her much more than curiosity about the rest of the world or even her past. What she'd learned and remembered so far about herself wasn't exactly reassuring, either. "When did you start painting?"

"I did watercolors when I was a child and a teen. My art teacher encouraged me to go to an art school. But I never imagined life away from the ranch. After high school, I worked full time here. There were always a lot of things to do. Important things. Animals are our livelihood, and we need to take care of them. Art seemed... trivial compared to that. One needed to feed stomachs before feeding souls. Two decades passed. Then I did a few paintings after watching internet videos. I didn't think about whether I was any good. It just felt... I needed to let out something that was swelling in my chest."

Hmm. He downplayed his talent, and it irked her just a little. Bringing people joy wasn't less important than feeding them, though as a person who didn't remember ever going hungry she was far from an expert on the subject.

"So most of your paintings are relatively recent. What changed?" She stroked the braids and picked up the bucket with brushes, then moved to the next stall, careful not to spook the horse.

"I met you."

Her hand with the brush stopped midair. "Oh. Am I your muse? I'm honored." She placed the brush back in the bucket, turned around, and walked to him as it dawned on her. "Did you... did you ever paint me?"

The tips of his ears reddened. "Yes, your face. I don't know if I was able to capture your beauty. But I had to paint you. I just couldn't... not do it."

"Well, if you did it with the same skill you painted landscapes and horses with, I'm sure I'll be impressed." She tilted her face. "Will you show me my portrait?"

"Of course." His fingertips touched the outline of her face, soft and tender like a paintbrush. "I wanted to give them to the exhibition in Springfield but not without your permission first. Beauty like yours belongs in an art gallery."

The admiration in his eyes pumped into her heart until her chest expanded. But then something rebelled in her. She was attracted to the real him while he, like many others before him, might've liked the beautiful picture, putting her on a pedestal. She didn't belong on a pedestal, in a museum—or in an art gallery, for that matter.

Living up to someone's high expectations wouldn't just be exhausting. It would be useless.

"I hope you don't create some unreachable ideal out of me. I'm a living, breathing woman with faults. Many faults."

"I realize that."

Did he, though? His brown eyes searched her. Was he memorizing her for another portrait?

He drew her close, and her heart fluttered. Was he going to kiss her at last? An inner struggle reflected in his features, and he let her go. Her gut knotted.

What was the matter? Did he prefer to admire her from afar rather than discover the real her and deal with her faults? Or was he hiding something? Or maybe both?

"What's wrong?" She challenged him more with her eyes than her words.

"I don't want to lose you." His voice rasped, and his eyes darkened.

Why would he lose her? There was something she didn't know. Correction: there were a lot of things she didn't know.

Two things were clear, though. One—she was falling for him fast and hard, be it for a hardworking cowboy or a talented artist who'd chosen her as his muse. Two—the things she didn't know had the ability to hurt her and most likely already had.

Chapter Ten

PANGS OF CONSCIENCE knifed at Brandon throughout dinner.

He should've told Madeline about their breakup. He should have! He shouldn't have agreed to pretend to be her boyfriend, even if for noble reasons.

He was going to tell her tonight. For sure, this time.

His gut twisted. She'd broken up with him when he hadn't given her any reason to. The chances of losing her when he had were much greater.

But as he passed the bread and thanked his mother and Madeline for cooking, a longing overwhelmed him. He'd learned a kinder, more vulnerable version of Madeline these days. It would be even more gut-wrenching to let that Madeline go.

She beamed as she praised his landscape, and he preened at the obvious pride in her voice. His longing intensified, and he hid it with a hurried sip of sweet tea.

He refilled her nearly empty glass from a pitcher. She wasn't just his dream girl. She was the dream. She was ephemeral like a morning mist, something to be admired, but impossible to hold onto. His heart shifted, refusing to accept it and let her go.

In a stunning silk dress the color of the sunrise, with her hair swept up in a sophisticated updo and her movements graceful, she belonged in a palace, not a ranch house. She was so different from his family so it should be jarring, like a rose in a wheat field.

Yet she fit here somehow. Her beautiful features were relaxed, and she carried on an easy conversation with his mother about some cake recipe.

Smiling broadly, Mom looked pleased. Most likely because of that, Dad grinned. Gratitude warmed Brandon as he gave the boiled bacon with cabbage and mashed potatoes its due. His father had gone through some rough times after breaking his leg and had sulked for a while. But now he was out and about again, though with a cane. He refused to use crutches. Being outside with the horses or tractors seemed to be the best medicine for him.

Jessie and Ronan still seemed to have eyes only for each other, and while Brandon was happy for his brother, a tiny sting of envy pinched like new cowboy boots that could rub skin raw until he got used to them.

Genevieve and her daughter radiated a warmth Brandon couldn't help but bask in.

Unlike the rest of the people at the table, Madeline's foster sister Arianna seemed to be on edge in several senses. From Madeline's unlikely family of the heart of five foster sisters, Brandon knew Arianna the least and understood her the least, too. Her dark hair fell over her eyes sometimes like a curtain to hide behind. Her black pantsuit was elegant but a sharp contrast to Madeline's peach dress and Genevieve's warm marmalade sweater. Arianna smiled and chatted, but he sensed it was a pretense for Madeline's sake. If Genevieve was a clear spring in the sunshine, Arianna was an ocean in Antarctica, with so much hidden under the surface.

The way Madeline used to be. But now she seemed like a river flowing along green banks, once chained in ice but now sparkling in the spring sun. And he didn't just say that because tiny diamond studs in her ears caught the light from the lamp above the table.

Arianna's eyes changed every time she talked to Madeline or about her, becoming a deeper shade of green, revealing genuine affection. But Arianna's gaze whenever she glanced at Brandon was assessing. He tensed. Did he pass the test?

Then Kieran's and Arianna's hands met when they reached toward the bread basket at the same time.

Arianna's hand froze midair. "Go ahead."

Kieran's neck pinked above his Wrangler's shirt. "No, you go ahead. Please."

"Thanks." She turned to his father and engaged him in conversation about tractors, oblivious to Kieran's reaction to their touch.

Kieran's gaze lingered on her. He seemed to forget he'd been reaching for something minutes ago. Or did he want to reach for something different now? Something perhaps unattainable?

From Madeline, Brandon knew Arianna wasn't going to stay in Cowboy Crossing. And if she did, she seemed to be worlds apart from his brother. Oceans apart.

Madeline hid a satisfied smile as she looked from Arianna to Kieran and back to Arianna. Uh-oh. Did she want those two to get together?

While Kieran appeared flustered, Arianna remained unreadable. Brandon pressed his lips flat, clamping in his thoughts. Was his brother heading to

Heartbreakville again? Brandon had been a resident there before, and it wasn't a good place to be.

Worse, he might be going back there again. The bacon soured in his stomach. But he had to be honest and tell Madeline the truth. The recent wonderful moments they'd shared and the affection she'd started looking at him with now—they all were stolen.

He could only hope she'd still let him protect her. So far, most of her suitors on the list had been cleared. But, despite Ronan's efforts, Matt Luettgen hadn't been found.

So after dinner and after everyone had helped to clean up, Madeline and Brandon volunteered to put dishes in the dishwasher, and he joined her in the kitchen.

He ran a hand over his poufy hair and swallowed hard. His palms were clammy when he pulled on yellow rubber gloves, and he didn't remember the last time he'd been this nervous. He didn't remember *ever* being this nervous. Which wasn't fair because she was the one who'd lost her memory. "We need to talk."

She whirled around and would've bumped into him if he didn't steady her. "Okay, this doesn't sound good. What happened?"

He drew a deep breath. Her signature lavender scent affected his senses, but he had to move past that. He had to do this. He took a deep breath and pushed out the confession. "I'm not your boyfriend. You broke up with me."

The plate slipped from her hands and shattered on the tile.

He suppressed a groan. He should've waited until she put down that plate. Plus a few years, give or take.

His mother poked her head into the kitchen. But, when he gave her a slight headshake, her eyes narrowed, and she retreated.

"You... can't be serious." Madeline crouched near the shards. Her fingers trembled.

"I'll take care of the plate." He strode to pick up the broom and dustpan from the closet, cowardly using the delay.

When he came back, she held shards in her hands, her face paler than its usual alabaster shade. Blood dripped from her fingers.

Oh no. She'd cut herself again!

She looked like a different person from the joyful woman at dinner. She'd looked happy then. Now the light had clouded over in her eyes, and ice encased the river again.

A chill sliced through him. What had he done? Had he made the biggest mistake of his life by telling her the truth?

He rushed to her and helped her up. "You're bleeding. Why did you try to pick up the shards with your bare hands?"

"I didn't think. Or maybe deep inside I knew it would hurt less. Pain and love often go together like two sisters, don't they?" She looked up at him, her blue eyes as shattered as the plate. "Arianna told me I used to cut myself. Did you know that?"

He shook his head. Not that it changed his opinion about her, except he understood now that she'd felt much more than she'd let on. He turned on the faucet and brought her fingers to the stream of water.

"Apparently, my foster sisters used to clean up my cuts. Tell me it would get better. But strangely, if I cut myself, that night I wouldn't have a nightmare. I'm an emotional mess, right? Is that why we broke up?" Her voice sounded hollow as if coming from some void inside her.

"No. You're not a mess. And... you never gave me a reason for the breakup." That had made it all so much worse. How was he supposed to change something if he didn't know what that was? He'd had his guesses at the time, afraid he'd just been another person in a long line of suitors she'd played and discarded. He knew better now. There was a second guess, too. "I thought maybe this place and I weren't sophisticated and good enough for you."

Instead of leaving to bring the first aid kit, he led her to it. He didn't want her to be alone.

Her mirthless laugh cut into him as he smeared antibiotic ointment on her cuts. "I don't need sophisticated. As for not being good enough, you're the best man I've ever met."

His chest swelled as he spread a waterproof Band-Aid across her palm. Then he reminded her and himself, "You don't remember any other men you dated."

"They couldn't have been better than you."

"Except for lying to you."

"Yes. Why did you do that?" She searched his eyes, more vulnerable than he'd ever seen her.

Seeing her like this broke his heart, and he only had himself to blame. "I said I was your boyfriend with sarcasm—and yeah, some wishful thinking. Then, when there was a possibility your life was in danger, I wanted to protect you. To help you recover."

She grimaced, twisting her lovely face up into pained lines. "That's not a good explanation. You could've done those things as a friend."

His stomach clenched. She had a point. He might as well say the main reason. "And in a more selfish part, I didn't want to lose you."

She pinned him with her gaze. "What if I regained my memory? I mean, all my memories?"

"It was worth it to be with you for whatever time I could rather than not being with you at all. You were worth it. Still are."

Eyes like hers could pierce one's soul. "It still doesn't excuse you lying to me."

"I'm not trying to find excuses. I'll understand if you'll never want to speak to me again." Everything inside him rebelled against that, but he deserved it.

"Was this the reason you didn't kiss me yet? Besides that chaste kiss in the hospital I asked for?"

"Yes. It seemed dishonest to kiss you. Well, more dishonest than what I'd already done." He cringed, his shoulders inching up by his ears. "I'm sorry."

Her eyes turned blank, and she became like a marble statue again. "I need to go."

"I'll follow you home."

She plastered on a smile as she walked outside the kitchen and said goodbye to his parents in the hall, but it wobbled at the sides. She didn't look at him once as she got into her car. Her shoulders slumped forward, and it made the guilt pressing down on his weigh a ton.

He followed her to the lodge, then past the gate, parked, and walked her inside. Arianna met them. Then her eyes narrowed, and she disappeared to her room as if giving them privacy.

Grateful for that, he stepped to Madeline. "Please give me another chance."

His heart seemed to stop beating while he waited for her answer.

She looked past him. "I... I need to process this. You were my world, and now that world tilted on its axis. I need to figure out what to do next."

"Would you let me be in your life at least as a friend?" He had to keep her safe somehow.

Her cell phone rang in her purse, and he nearly groaned.

"Sorry." She reached for it, then frowned. "I don't know this name." She hesitated. "Of course, *I* don't remember any names."

"Please don't mind me. Go ahead and find out who that is."

She answered the call.

Her eyes were huge when she disconnected. "It's a private investigator. Apparently, I hired her to investigate the murder of my parents. She wants to meet me tomorrow."

The next day, Madeline's mind still reeled as she let the PI inside and introduced her to Brandon. Had her attack indeed been connected to the decades-old crime? Had someone felt threatened because she set things in motion?

Of course, the new dynamic of her relationship with Brandon rattled her much worse. How could he mislead her like that?

With her new reality so shaky, he'd been the only stable thing left. She'd thought they'd walked on common ground. Instead, she'd been walking on ice that threatened to break. His betrayal already felt like icy water numbed her limbs, made it hard to function. Both men dear to her had betrayed her.

What was wrong with her?

Her past was a mystery. Now so was her present.

Brandon touched her forearm in silent support as they walked to the living room, and she had to remind herself not to lean in his direction. She'd grown so used to relying on him that she needed him like air. But a lie had polluted the air she'd considered fresh and clear.

He did have good intentions, though. But thinking like that could make her slip and go under the ice.

She had to stay in the moment. She had to concentrate on the investigation she'd started.

The private investigator was nothing like she'd expected. But her idea of PIs was based on the noir movie she and Brandon had recently seen together.

Jenna looked more like a femme fatale than the middle-aged man in a fedora and trench coat. She drew immediate attention with electric-blue eyes and a tall, slim body hugged by a fashionable white pantsuit. The elegant diamond-shaped buckle on the belt cinching her ensemble tight somehow matched the chunky earrings dangling beneath her short jet-black hair. Even shorter than Jessie wore hers, Jenna's hair offered a striking contrast to those eyes, and long bangs swept to the side gave it a stylish cut.

Madeline did her best to ignore a sting of envy. While she liked expensive clothes in no particular order, Jenna had a unique fashion style that somehow looked effortless. Madeline had done a little research about Jenna yesterday, but she didn't have to go far.

Since Brandon knew Jenna, who was a local, Madeline had reluctantly probed him as her source of information. Jenna was born on the neighboring ranch and was the veterinarian Liberty's sister. Unlike her siblings, Jenna had lived in Europe for a long time and worked there as an art theft investigator. Since coming home, she'd married her family's ranch foreman and adopted the nephew he'd been raising, all after she'd solved his sister's murder and rescued his nephew. This woman was remarkable in more than her appearance.

Now Jenna and her husband had a toddler. Together with two other women in their large family, Jenna had formed an all-female detective agency. Based on the online reviews, they had a great reputation.

Once again, the image didn't mesh with Madeline's already preconceived notion of a private investigator, but she did her best not to be sexist.

She gestured for them to take seats, and Brandon joined her on the sofa, which left the armchair to Jenna. Madeline perched on the edge, supporting herself with the cute pink and blue throw pillows by the armrest.

"Let me start by saying I found the email communication with you, but I don't remember hiring you." Madeline winced. That didn't sound right.

Before she could continue, Jenna nodded. "I'd be bad at what I do if I didn't know about your amnesia." She opened the briefcase she carried and handed Madeline a folder. "Here's our contract. We can stop the investigation, or we can continue. It's up to you."

Madeline liked the directness. She leafed through the contract, handed the folder back, and made a decision fast, surprising herself. "I want to continue."

"Okay." Jenna slipped the folder back into the briefcase, not sounding surprised. Emotions didn't flicker over her striking face. "It doesn't mean we'll solve the crime."

Again, Jenna's directness appealed. "I understand. But at least we can try." She'd avoided looking into her past long enough. Now when she had one huge gap instead of years of memories, she wanted to know.

Do you really want to do it? Jenna didn't ask that question, but it flashed in those electric eyes.

Brandon had asked that yesterday when she'd been ferreting Jenna's information from him. Several times.

The answer was always the same. Madeline didn't want to, but she chose to. She'd draw the line at looking at photos of the crime scene. The images in her mind would become gut-wrenching if she could recall all of them.

The idea was... abstract, maybe? Almost as if she was watching someone else's story unfold. But, even if she didn't know why she'd started this investigation before her memory loss, there had to be a valid reason. Had she recalled something important about that tragic night?

Chapter Eleven

FAMILIAR WORDS ECHOED in Madeline's mind.

Sorry, Daddy.

Sorry I didn't save you.

Of course, digging into the cold case could've caused that attack on her. She shivered, and Brandon drew his arm around her protectively.

She wanted so badly to drink strength from him. Still, she straightened her spine and shifted away, and his arm dropped. She wasn't a one-dimensional romantic portrait. She could do this.

She leaned forward. "What have you been able to find?"

Jenna gave her a gaze filled with a hint of compassion. Compassion and not pity because surely she guessed Madeline wouldn't tolerate pity. Then she picked up a different folder from her briefcase and gave it to Madeline. "I'll send you full reports, as well, so you'll have a digital copy. Right now, I'll start from the beginning. Your parents were killed in their sleep between midnight and two o'clock. Your mother was killed first, which is unusual."

Madeline tried to think of her parents as strangers in this case. It was easier that way. "A man was a bigger threat. Technically, he'd be killed first."

Something akin to respect accompanied Jenna's nod. "Correct. The murder weapon was a 38mm gun. You were all at a vacation lake house, so there were no neighbors to hear the shots."

No neighbors. "Who reported it?" Madeline could guess the answer before she asked it. She didn't open the folder yet.

"You did. You were in shock and just a child, but you were coherent."

"Why was I spared?" Her mouth and lips felt dry, but she stayed pinned in place instead of going to get water.

Brandon spoke up as if reading her mind. "Would anyone like something to drink?"

Madeline should've offered that already. But her mind was too rattled for her to pose as a good hostess. Her fingers trembled, and she laced them together. She wasn't sure she could bring glasses without spilling water or juice everywhere.

Jenna declined, but Madeline croaked, barely recognizing her voice, "Water, please."

While he left and water ran in the kitchen, Madeline's eyes glazed, the fireplace beside Jenna's chair blurring. Then he came back with a tall glass, and she gulped it down greedily. Yesterday, he'd told her that, if she went through with this investigation, her world was never going to be the same.

But he didn't understand. Her world was never going to be the same, anyway.

She could guess why she'd avoided looking into her parents' double homicide. She'd wanted to hold onto that picture-perfect snapshot of her family she'd given the girls. A well-respected, admired doctor and his devoted, beautiful wife.

Life rarely was like that. A lot of things were an illusion, like Brandon being her boyfriend and being true to her. What if she was about to send that perfect family photo to the floor, its glass covering shattering into pieces that cut her? She looked at her palm with fresh Band-Aids. She'd already had too many cuts, some hidden like those on her stomach or on her heart. Some in broad view like those on her palm.

Another thought wormed inside. Why hadn't she asked Jessie to help with the investigation? Did something in Jessie's behavior prompt even a kernel of doubt? Or was it because Jessie was busy with her new job and her new married life? Jenna could easily travel to Houston while Jessie—not so much. And Jessie had come into Madeline's life way after Madeline's parents' murder. Madeline breathed a little easier.

She badly needed people in her life she could rely on. Arianna wasn't much for emotional support, so Madeline had spent the evening crying on Genevieve's shoulder while Jessie and Arianna kept bringing tissues.

"Were there any suspects?" Madeline's voice sounded stronger, but still foreign.

"Yes." Letting out a deep breath, Jenna crossed her legs and settled back in her chair. "One of your father's patients died, and the patient's father blamed your dad. He had an alibi at the time, though. He spent the night of the murder at his friend's place, drinking."

Madeline filed it in the mostly empty room that her memory was. "Were you able to interview that suspect?"

Jenna shook her head, sending her spectacular bangs flying. "No. He died five years ago in his sleep."

Brandon stiffened, seeming to pick up on something Madeline hadn't. "You said 'alibi *at the* time.'"

A fly bumped into the window, trying to get in, not realizing that, once it did, it would be trapped inside. Was Madeline just like that fly, going where she wasn't supposed to, about to pay for it if she succeeded?

"I talked to the person who provided the alibi." Jenna's calm voice snapped Madeline's attention back. "After some time, he admitted he wasn't with the suspect then."

Brandon shifted closer. "How did you manage to achieve that?"

Jenna shrugged, and her upper lip moved slightly in an expression that on someone less sophisticated would look feral. "I have great persuasion skills. Besides, over three decades later and with his friend gone, it mattered less now. I said I wouldn't report him."

Hmm. Madeline regretted not starting the investigation sooner, but maybe in some senses, it could work to their advantage. People might be more forthcoming with information now. Less protective of the secrets that could've been eroding their conscience for such a long time.

Her entire past was a secret to her, though not as much now as when she'd woken up in the hospital. Whatever time she hadn't spent with Brandon, she'd been painstakingly reconstructing the person she was in her mind as if creating a collection of large paintings with tiny beads. Did she use the right beads in the right places, though?

She'd spent lots of time searching files on her phone and laptop, paperwork, and social media. She'd spent even more time with people who knew her well, like Jessie, Arianna, and Genevieve. But she had to account for the fact that their perception of her had been filtered through their lenses. In Genevieve's case, the lens of kindness and nearly maternal love glossed over everything. Madeline suspected she and her foster sisters had survived their difficult childhoods mostly due to Genevieve.

Paisley was just as sweet during her conference calls from Germany. The "beads" they had given Madeline had been sparkly and clean and pretty. Arianna was the most objective. Her recollection beads came with a few jagged edges. But Madeline felt those parts of the picture of her past fit for sure. Arianna had a few serrated edges to herself, as well.

The most joyful information source by far was Brandon's Post-its. But maybe his notes were a bit too bright and cheerful like the paper he'd written on. In them, she was beautiful like the sunrise-tinted roses he'd brought her.

The person who'd cut into people as part of her job and cut into her own skin as a teen was far from cheerful. The person who'd found her parents in a pool of blood wasn't sunrise and roses.

Maybe not knowing was a blessing. Maybe she should take on the persona Genevieve and Brandon were offering her.

She realized her thoughts had drifted off when Jenna's gaze sharpened and the silence stretched between them. Brandon sent Madeline a worried glance as if asking her whether she was okay. Had she tuned out because she didn't want to hear what Jenna had said?

Madeline lifted her chin. She could do this. She could. "Sorry. What did you say?"

Hands folded calmly in her lap, Jenna met her gaze head-on, and only the barely noticeable tightness of her lips showed her discomfort. "Your mother had an affair with her former boyfriend."

Madeline flinched and lifted her hands as if she wanted to shield herself from the news. Here it was. What she didn't want to hear. The porcelain figurine was not only shattered but thrown into the mud. "Are you sure?" How could Jenna know?

"Our detective agency maintains a system of networks with other private investigators across the country and even the world. I put out some feelers in Houston and got a call from a retired PI. Your father hired him to follow your mother."

Madeline's breath lodged in her throat and stayed there kicking and screaming before she could drag it into her lungs. "So... do you think my father knew?"

"The PI was going to turn in his report on Monday. But the day before..." Jenna shrugged. She didn't need to explain.

"Dad suspected something. Or he wouldn't have hired a PI." Madeline drew a shaky breath of air now tainted with suspicion. Then another thought struck and stole her breath again. "And he had a motive for murder."

Strangely, a happier memory appeared in her mind. Her running barefoot in the hall, screaming "Daddy!" Him stepping into the hall, lifting her up. She'd been laughing then. Her mother walked to them in a peach-hued apron, beaming. Mom smelled of a pie, and her smile was luminous as she moved close for a three-person hug.

"I love you, Daddy. I love you, Mommy." Madeline had felt protected and safe then. And very much loved.

"It wasn't murder-suicide," Jenna said, bringing Madeline to the present. "No murder weapon was found nearby. Blood splatter trajectory shows both shots were made from a distance to the respective victims."

Blood splatter trajectory.

It sounded so... so cold. But so was Madeline. She shivered but didn't get up for a jacket. Her legs likely wouldn't carry her, anyway.

Brandon ran his hands over her arms. "Would you like me to bring you something warm?"

She shook her head. The cold came from within. A blanket wouldn't help.

Was she cold that horrifying day, too? Arianna had told Madeline the police found her in the forest that morning, shivering in her pajamas. She couldn't stay in the house with dead bodies. No, wrong.

Her father's moving lips. But she couldn't remember a sound. He'd probably asked for help. But like a coward, she'd run away to the forest, leaving him to die. Maybe that had been the reason she'd cut herself as a child. Guilt and not grief. She'd needed to punish herself.

You're a disappointment.

She needed to concentrate on the new suspect. "What happened to that former boyfriend? Did he have a fake alibi, as well?"

"I haven't been able to crack his alibi so far. He married and had three children. Seven grandchildren."

"What a family man." Maybe sarcasm was unwarranted, but Madeline couldn't help herself. "Was he married at the time of the affair, too?"

Her ideal of a happy family shattered. Was there any hope for her and Brandon? Could she trust him? He'd hid an important part of their relationship from her. While she'd agreed to give him a second chance as a friend this morning, it was out of pure desperation. Once broken, trust wasn't easily repaired.

Some things couldn't be glued together.

She concentrated on breathing in and out. The happy family in the photo album she'd treasured throughout the years was an illusion.

But then, weren't all memories an illusion, good things people perceived to be true? Or was it the opposite, that bad things usually came to the forefront of the mind? Like how even though Brandon had done so much for her, she couldn't forget that he'd hidden their breakup from her.

Breathe.

Think about the case.

"How did the perp get inside?" Madeline asked.

Jenna nodded in approval as if she considered the question a good one. "The lock wasn't tampered with. Neither was the security system."

The words registered, then sliced through her. "So whoever did it had the key? Knew codes to the alarm system?"

"Or had a copy of the key," Jenna suggested.

So most likely it wasn't someone random or a patient's traumatized relative, though Madeline didn't remove that person from the suspect list.

"Fingerprints?" She didn't put much stock in the question. Even over three decades ago, people knew to use gloves.

Jenna shook her head.

So it was someone close to the family. Close people who pretended to care could be an illusion, as well.

"I'm going through the list of friends and relatives who might know the alarm codes. I did several interviews and will send you the report. As your parents were both only children and distant relatives lived far away, the second list is way shorter than the first one," Jenna said.

Madeline was helpless concerning both lists. Why hadn't she started this when she'd still had her childhood memories? She ground her molars. She knew the answer to that question, but that didn't mean she had to like it.

"Tell me about my parents." She ground her molars tighter. Having to ask such a question irked her. She must be the only person for many miles who didn't have a clue about what her parents were like. Now she understood how Jessie and Paisley felt while growing up. Jessie still didn't know who her father was.

At least, Madeline had photos, but so many secrets could linger behind smiles and loving glances.

Jenna's gaze softened. "Everyone I talked to described your mother as a sociable, outgoing person. She was well liked, and people were drawn to her. Before her marriage, she worked as a cashier at a grocery store, and her colleagues said she had an easy laugh and a caring personality that was always ready to help. According to her neighbors, she often invited them for a cup of tea or brought them pie."

Madeline could almost smell and taste a peach cobbler again. She should've been pleased her mom's nice characteristics weren't all in her imagination. But she could only think about how she hadn't gotten her keep-people-at-a-distance nature from her mother.

"She doted on you." Despite the sweet words, Jenna's mouth tightened as if she'd bit into something unpleasant.

Guessing what was coming, Madeline tensed.

Brandon moved closer to her as if sensing her increasing dread.

"What about my father?"

There it was again. The tightness of Jenna's lips wouldn't have been noticeable if Madeline hadn't paid such attention. "He kept to himself and worked long hours. He was… conservative and career-oriented."

Did that translate to saying he didn't pay enough attention to his family? Was her mother lonely? Was the real reason behind inviting her neighbors for tea and taking them pies so they'd have no other choice but to reciprocate the invitation?

That wasn't a question for Jenna, at least not yet.

But a part of Madeline could understand her father. She had difficulty relating to people, at least alive ones, hence her career choice. According to her foster sisters, she'd spent too much time at work, too. Yes, she was close to her foster sisters, but it could be because they hadn't allowed her to push them away. Maybe what she'd wanted was to be accomplished, not liked.

Was her mother the opposite way? Or was it because she'd fallen in love with the wrong person for her?

Would the light have gone out of her mother's eyes in time because of that? Madeline stole a glance at Brandon. Would she do the same to him? He deserved to have someone like her mother, joyful and radiant.

Even her mother's appearance with a blonde bob and sparkling light-blue eyes confirmed that. Madeline got her dark hair from her father. He had dominant genes in several senses.

Apparently, Madeline didn't know how to be radiant, how to show love, how to spread cheer. That lunch with Brandon when she'd licked her fingers and stolen his fries seemed so far away. Maybe it wasn't in her genes. She was her father's daughter.

Not that one couldn't be well liked and accomplished at the same time. Her foster sister Paisley was a prime example. With a brilliant mind, Paisley was successful in her field, but people were also drawn to her sunny attitude. Sadly, despite their lifetime of friendship, that sunny attitude hadn't rubbed off on Madeline.

Jenna got up and smoothed down her slacks.

Madeline's mind must have drifted off again.

"That's all I have for now." Jenna paused before asking the question Madeline dreaded. "I realize this was a lot of painful information. So I'm asking again. Do you want me to continue the investigation?"

Her first impulse was to shake her head. But her parents deserved justice, and she'd avoided her responsibility of helping find it for way too long. She'd already failed her father too many times. By breaking his porcelain figurine. By not continuing his legacy and becoming a surgeon. By abandoning him when he'd needed her the most.

Her lungs seemed to burn as if she were running through a forest again in the darkness. She'd tripped over a tree root, fallen, scratched her palms that smarted, then scrambled to her feet and run again, tasting her salty tears. She'd been complaining that her ex and Brandon had betrayed her, but she was a much worse traitor, and her father had paid a high price for her betrayal.

Could she have saved him if she'd stayed and pressed some fabric into the wound to stop the bleeding? She'd never know. But he'd obviously tried to tell her the name of the person who'd shot him and Mom. Madeline could've at least brought them justice then. But she hadn't stayed to listen, had she?

A disappointment. That was too soft a word for someone like her.

Was it a mistake to find the truth now? Like it was a mistake to let Brandon into her life again, even as a friend?

She'd told herself she'd needed him because of the circumstances, because she didn't want to put her foster sisters in danger. But it was much more than that.

Her heart fluttered. She wanted him to be more than a friend. Her entire being was drawn to him like a magnet, even now, when she knew about their breakup. But she'd be naïve to hope for a second—no, wait, a third—chance.

Brandon squeezed her fingers as if to support either decision. The simple gesture sent a jolt of awareness straight to her heart.

"Yes. Please continue with the investigation," she told Jenna, hoping she wouldn't regret it.

Knowing she probably would.

Chapter Twelve

BRANDON'S HEAD SPUN as he groomed the horses for the upcoming parade tomorrow. Every year, his family participated in the town parade and held a few fundraisers and entertainment events.

The familiar activity helped calm his raw nerves.

Because not only was he completely out of his element, first dating Madeline and now being her friend, but also this murder investigation puzzled him. Unlike his cop brother, Brandon had never been intrigued by mysteries and solving crimes. Working at the ranch, raising cattle and taking care of horses, helping his brothers achieve their dreams, and continuing the legacy of what had been in his family for generations had been all he'd ever wanted.

Until he'd met Madeline.

If stopping himself from hugging and kissing her when she'd believed him to be her boyfriend had been difficult, now it was torture. She suggested they be friends now, and he'd agreed because he'd rather have her in his life as a friend than not at all.

Yet he was falling for her. Not the cold beauty he'd first met and only glimpsed kindness and vulnerability in, but the woman with a fun side and a hurting soul he'd discovered since her amnesia.

"I'll end up with a broken heart again, much more painful this time," he told Speckles.

The beautiful Appaloosa neighed as if agreeing with him. She lifted her graceful neck and peered at him with her dewy eyes, perhaps wondering why he would stay in a doomed relationship.

"I can't walk away, either," he replied to his thoughts and maybe the horse's, too. "She means too much to me. And she needs me."

That was the thing about people in this family. They needed to be needed. By people. By ranch animals. Even by the land they'd grown up on.

"I knew I'd find you here." Madeline's voice made him whirl around.

Based on the noise behind him, they'd startled the Appaloosa, so the quick movement wasn't a good idea. Yet he stayed rooted in place instead of calming the horse. Just the sight of Madeline made his heart stutter.

"I brought ribbons." She lifted bright blue and pink ribbons. "To put in the horses' manes. Make them look pretty."

Only Madeline would think of that. But she had a knack for making things more beautiful by her mere presence.

Well, nothing mere about it.

The wildflower bouquet she'd picked for the family dinner table had been well put together. She had an eye for things that complemented each other. Her dress style was something this town had never seen before in real life. The wedding cake she'd created for Paisley's hasty wedding was a masterpiece, and she'd been the one to point out where each of the decorations went.

Just like their private investigator, Madeline had an innate sense of style. Though, where Jenna had gone for originality, Madeline went for classic elegance. Neither one seemed born for ranch life.

He didn't think horses needed embellishments. But he'd stared at her for too long without speaking, so he nodded as he took the ribbons and placed them aside. "Thank you."

Those two words didn't encompass everything he felt.

I missed you so much.

I ache to hold you.

I get lost in the blue ocean of your eyes and don't want to come back ashore.

A friend couldn't say those things, so he just asked, "Are you okay?"

Not the best thing to ask, either. She wasn't okay. How could she be, discovering a worrisome secret about her family that already had a tragic past?

But that was his way to show her he cared without touching her. He wanted to, so badly he had to shove his hands into his pockets to stop from reaching out to her.

"No. But I'm trying to be." She started braiding the horse that already knew her.

He paused in his work to finger through his hair and make sure the silly cut was in its proper place, hating this awkwardness between them now and aching to whisk it away.

Great. He was supposed to be grooming the horses, not himself. He ground his teeth. His memory did him a disservice, though, as he continued currying the Appaloosa, reminding him how Madeline had looked at him with trust and admiration, how she'd hugged him, how he'd melted carrying her in his arms after her car accident.

His heart twisted further, wrenching more painfully this time. Had he ruined it all by taking advantage of her amnesia and pretending to be her boyfriend?

He had only himself to blame.

"What can I do to help?" He stayed in place, now working with the next brush because, if he as much as looked at her, he wouldn't be able to resist the pull she had on him.

She was like his personal whirlpool, the currents not allowing him to swim away. "You're already helping me. By... by tolerating me. I realize I'm not the easiest person to be around. I'm not sunshine like Paisley. I'm not an open and nourishing field like you. I'm a thunderstorm ready to drench people in their own tears even if I don't intend to."

So her distance wasn't just because of what he'd done but also because of the things she'd been finding out about herself? About the tragedy of her family?

"Every family has secrets," he said carefully. He was out of his element here, too. His family life was simple.

"Not yours." No envy tinged her voice, just admiration.

He was grateful for his steady family. Like his brothers, he'd taken his family for granted until he'd met Madeline and her foster sisters. That all of these women not only survived but also became successful was remarkable. He was proud to call two of them his sisters-in-law now.

"It's not only about a family by blood. It's about the family of the heart. And you have that," he said.

"I do have that." Her head tipped up, slippery hair gliding over her shoulders as surprise rang in her words as if that gift puzzled her.

He'd seen her caring side with her foster sisters, her dog, and now with these horses. But he guessed she was afraid to show that side to other people.

It wasn't about genetics. Brandon didn't need to be a psychologist to see that it was a response to childhood trauma. Her world had been horrifically upended when she'd been little.

Would revisiting those events make things worse for her? He said a prayer for her. Then for himself, for Madeline to forgive him and for God to guide him to help her because, so far, he had no clue how.

Madeline didn't like crowds. They made her feel suffocated, or at least, they did now.

Too many unfamiliar faces, and she didn't know which she was supposed to recognize. Too many scents assaulting her at the parade the next day.

Besides, what if the person who'd hit her on the head decided to repeat the gesture and disappear into the crowd? On the other hand, a second hit might return her memory rather than make it worse, but that wasn't the way she wanted to find out.

Well, it was a beautiful day with lots of sunshine. And fine, the main reason she was in the crowded town square right now was because she didn't want to miss the sight of Brandon.

His posture, his confidence, and the way he stood out with his bay Thoroughbred made her chest swell.

A small part of her wished she still believed he was her boyfriend, that they were still together. She missed the feeling of belonging, basking in his admiration, his support. So much for her apparent independence. She pulled back her shoulders, feigning that confidence. She had to find her footing, and the sooner the better.

Arianna shifted toward her. Ronan and Jessie were working, providing security for the parade, or they'd be here, as well. Genevieve was laughing with her daughter as they stood with their arms linked while watching the band, floats, and horses.

Arianna's attention was on the crowd. Her taut-set lips and her eyes, a darker shade of green than usual, now the color of pine trees in the rain, revealed she didn't like crowds, either. She could be sociable if she wanted to be, but Madeline knew by now it came at an effort. The only time Arianna didn't seem on guard was at their lodge, and while Madeline often wondered what had honed that skill, she wouldn't ask.

A truck-pulled float lumbered by. Teens in their school colors on the float trailer tossed candy to the kids in the crowd, their high school mascot waved while people shouted "Go, Mustangs!"

Madeline's attention returned to Brandon down a side street, visible, but well away from where the noisy band was getting ready to march. He and his brother Sean waited, fully geared in cowboy boots, chaps, and Stetsons and prepared to ride down the street on immaculately groomed, perfectly matched bay Thoroughbreds, each leading a string of the ponies they'd be giving rides on this afternoon.

"Would you ladies like some coffee?" Kieran made it to them through the crowd. Though he asked both of them, he focused on Arianna. Did he have a crush on her?

Madeline hid a smile, pleased for her friend.

"Thanks." Arianna took the coffee, but her gaze slid over him way too fast, as if dismissing him.

Disappointment flickered in his eyes, and Madeline's heart squeezed. Maybe she shouldn't be so pleased for her foster sister. Arianna didn't see the treasure the O'Neill brothers were.

Or maybe she didn't want to give false promises. She'd admitted she never stayed in one place long. Some restlessness about her kept driving her on.

The marching band started down the street, brass instruments shining and silvery batons twirling. Lifting onto tiptoe—as if she could stand even taller than she already was in her high-heeled boots—Madeline craned to see how Brandon was keeping those horses and ponies calm through the chaotic sound.

A shove to her shoulder nearly sent her to the ground, but Arianna broke her fall. Then, as Madeline wobbled on her high heels, her purse was torn from her shoulder, and some guy in a cap and jeans took off with it.

"Stop!" Madeline screamed but didn't give chase. With those high-heeled boots and her lack of athleticism, such pursuit would be useless.

Arianna and Kieran didn't have the same issue. They sprinted through the crowd after the guy. Her heart thudding faster than the approaching drums, Madeline followed at a much slower speed. Was this her attacker? Would they solve the mystery of the assault in the park now?

Kieran tackled the guy to the ground before Arianna had a chance to, which likely disappointed her.

"Let me go!" The guy flailed.

Kieran scrambled to his feet, keeping a wary eye on the thief.

Ronan and Jessie elbowed through the crowd, and Ronan pulled the guy up.

Kieran handed Madeline her purse, but his attention switched back to Arianna. He must've hoped to impress her. Instead, she looked irritated.

"Madeline, could you please check if everything is there?" Jessie asked. In other times, she'd probably hug Madeline, but now she was professionalism personified.

Madeline did so and nodded. "I don't think anything is missing."

On a closer look, the culprit appeared to be around sixteen, way shorter than she was, and on the skinny side as if his limbs were growing faster than the rest of his body. Those holes in his jeans seemed to be from age, not a fashion statement.

Compassion stirred in her belly, and she stepped closer. "Why did you do this?"

Shrugging, the kid looked away. "That's a nice purse."

Yes, it was. It was a designer bag, and she had several. The band marched along, mere feet away, the music drowning out all but the blood rushing in her ears. Light with relief, she let out her pent-up breath, her adrenaline ebbing away. So it wasn't anything personal. Or at least she wanted to believe that. Someone could've hired the teen.

Even more, she wanted to believe the assault in the park hadn't been personal. In the same logic, she'd worn nice jewelry.

Maybe someone like Arianna could live constantly looking over their shoulder, was used to it even, but Madeline didn't want to live that way. Or were these two different scenarios? Besides, pickpockets were common in a crowd, weren't they?

Brandon made it to her and hugged her, and she let him.

Then his body angled toward the teen. "Tommy?"

Shuffling his scuffed sneakers, the boy scowled at the ground and didn't say anything. Even with his shoulders hunched, defiance radiated from his posture.

As Brandon's body tensed, Madeline loosened her grip on him and pulled back enough to see his face. With the band having passed, she could almost hear again, and the name sounded familiar. "Is that Tommy?"

Brandon nodded, his eyes dulling with a hollowness. "He's one of the teens who work at the nearby ranch. I work with them sometimes on a volunteer basis."

One of the troubled teens. Brandon had omitted that part. He'd told her about the program they started as a summer camp for foster teens and how it evolved to a place for troubled teens where they could work with horses and work off the steam. All the teens there came from difficult families where their parents either didn't care about their children or left altogether.

She slid her arms from Brandon's waist and palmed her hair from her face, raising her chin with a quick decision. "I'm not going to press charges."

"Are you sure?" Jessie asked, but her gray eyes softened already. As much as she professed her affinity for justice, she had a compassionate side, as well.

"Yes."

The boy's body sagged. Then he frowned at Brandon. "Am I gonna be kicked out of the program?" With the slightest beseeching in his posture, he looked more worried about that scenario than going to jail.

"I'll talk to the program manager. Were you going to sell this purse?" Brandon's focus zeroed in on him.

Head ducked down, Tommy didn't say anything. Then he scuffled his feet, nudging a pebble loose from the sidewalk crack with his sneaker. "No. A girl I like has a birthday tomorrow. She's never had a nice purse. She's got no parents."

Was it a sob story, or was it real? Call Madeline skeptical, but she hoped Brandon would verify it. But if it was true... Madeline could relate to the no-parents part. "You could've just asked for it. I'll empty it at home and bring it to you with a few other things."

The boy blinked. "Seriously?"

"Sure." She pushed her hair out of the way and slung the purse over her shoulder for now. "I'll also bake a birthday cake, though don't expect me to sing 'Happy Birthday' to her. That would scare her away."

He gawked at her. "You can bake?"

Brandon hugged her again. "You'd better believe it." The pride in his voice rang out as clear and bright as those passing brass cymbals. "She's amazing."

Then it dawned on her. With a hand on his shoulder, she leaned into him and whispered, "Did you abandon the parade?"

"A cowhand took my place. I was worried about you."

His concern warmed her heart. Who was she kidding? He meant more to her than a friend. Much more. That meant she had to ask for space from him. Try to keep her distance.

Right after the parade.

Chapter Thirteen

MADELINE GROANED and pushed back from her chair in the breakfast nook. She'd done her best not to miss Brandon. She'd tried to stay angry with him. But she couldn't. Every fiber of her being longed to be with him. And her memory, so reluctant to give up what had happened before the hit on the head, was generous with every minute she'd spent with Brandon afterward—and she'd given her memory plenty of those minutes to dwell on.

Hungry for distraction, she went to play catch with Rusty in the lodge's backyard so lush with spring greenery. It reminded her of Brandon and him bringing her to the lodge, helping her adjust to the place and even her dog. She stilled. Rusty nudged her hand with his wet nose, so she threw the ball again. She managed to give him an approving smile when he brought the ball back, but tears burned in the backs of her eyes.

She wouldn't cry. She absolutely wouldn't cry. Yet a few tears escaped.

Then Rusty's hackles rose, and he bared his teeth as he dashed to the fence. He stopped, and a low growl rumbled in his throat. She tensed as she followed.

Did he sense an intruder?

Her stomach clenched. She couldn't see through the fence, of course, so she fished out her phone from her jeans pocket and searched for outside camera footage. Okay. No hooded figure crouched beyond the fence, and she could breathe again.

Rusty stopped growling. His posture relaxed, and so did her stomach muscles. A squirrel hopped through the nearest tree branches, and Rusty gave out a bark.

"Was that all about a squirrel?" She laughed nervously.

Maybe she was jumpy. Well, no *maybe* about it. She picked up the salad-green ball and threw it to the other side of the yard. Rusty followed it in a flash. If only she had such energy.

While they hadn't renovated the lodge as a safe place specifically for her, she was grateful it had been done. She'd felt safe with Brandon wherever they'd gone, but not by herself, and he didn't want her to go anywhere by herself in the first place. She groaned again. Why did her thoughts keep returning to him?

"Good job." She gave Rusty a nice back rub when he brought the ball back. She'd take him to the pond later. Getting the ball from the water would give him a bigger challenge. Thankfully, Arianna had been taking him on her morning runs, or he'd have even more energy.

Rusty preened at her praise.

"At least you'll never betray me, right?" She looked into his dark eyes.

He barked, which hopefully meant she shouldn't even be asking that question. She eyed the fence again. She'd been in a house behind a high fence with a great security system before. Yet she'd been bound, robbed, and nearly killed. That knowledge, not some nonexistent memory, made her shudder, and Rusty licked her hand as if trying to lick her soul wounds.

But then, a person inside her house—inside her heart—betrayed her.

Brandon's offense wasn't anything close to that, and yet it hurt. It would've been easier to forgive him if he hadn't meant so much to her. But maybe his fibbing to her wasn't what caused her to pull back.

Try as she might, she wasn't disappointed in him. But she *was* disappointed in herself. In the way she floundered without purpose now. In the way she couldn't be as nice to people as they were to her. In the way she'd run away scared when her father had been shot and needed her help.

Was God disappointed in her, as well? Whatever purpose God had given her in life, she wasn't fulfilling it.

Unlike Brandon.

Even now, her fingers itched to call him. But how could she when she'd been the one to ask for space?

With the gray sky a match to her mood, the air grew humid and heavy. She walked to the patio doors, waving Rusty along. "It looks like it's going to rain. Let's go inside."

He gave a little whine, likely saying he didn't mind the rain, but he trudged behind her.

Once inside, she wiped his paws with a towel. "You know what? I'll give you a bath."

Rusty tilted his head and didn't look too excited. Huh. She'd probably even managed to disappoint her dog when she'd screamed the first time she'd seen him after getting amnesia. She'd have run away scared then, as well, if not for Brandon. Arianna had taken care of Rusty while Madeline had been in the hospital, and then Arianna had been helping out a lot, from taking him for runs to feeding him in the morning. Arianna was an early riser.

More guilt piled up, and Madeline sighed.

Bathing Rusty turned out to be a two-person job because Rusty didn't want to follow her to the bathroom. It could've been a four-person job if Genevieve and Gold weren't grocery shopping.

"This isn't supposed to be like this," Madeline said as Arianna dragged Rusty on the leash to the bathroom and Madeline pushed him from behind. Madeline considered sliding him on the hardwood floor, but that might leave scratches.

"Nope." Arianna grimaced.

"Do we have a skateboard?" If they could place Rusty on it, that would make things easier. Especially if he stayed on it.

Arianna glanced back. "Nope again, but it goes on my shopping list now." She maneuvered Rusty inside the bathroom.

"How did we do it before?" Grunting, Madeline helped her friend get her dog into the bathtub with Arianna doing most of the lifting. One of them needed to exercise more, and that someone wasn't Arianna or Rusty.

"Brandon carried Rusty." Arianna reached for the pet shampoo.

"Right." A memory filtered in. Brandon's arms around her as she looked up at him, his scent of musk and hay and leather clouding her senses. He'd carried her, too. Her treacherous heart fluttered. "How did I do it by myself before?"

Arianna shrugged. "Beats me. Brandon must've spoiled Rusty. I just hose him down outside after our morning runs." She coughed a little. "Hose down Rusty, not Brandon."

A chuckle escaped as Madeline shampooed Rusty's spectacular fur. "Yeah. I guessed." Though she wouldn't mind watching Arianna hose down Brandon with water... Her cheeks flamed.

Frankly, Brandon had spoiled her, too. He'd been by her side when she'd needed him the most, never asking for anything in return. First, after the car accident when she'd broken her wrist—the fact that she didn't remember it didn't make it any less valuable. Then, after her amnesia when she was confused and needy. Every one of his Post-its was etched into her memory. She could still taste the tacos he'd helped her make, smell the roses he'd brought, feel the tenderness in his hands when he'd bandaged her wounds.

He'd painted the world in bright colors for her again, in several senses.

How could she be angry with a man like that?

"Am I being too harsh with Brandon?" She touched Arianna's hand, pausing her as they dried Rusty. The German shepherd looked at them with sad eyes, and Madeline promised him a treat. But the kind of treat she wanted, simply to see Brandon, she couldn't have. Her gut twisted.

"Yes." Arianna didn't hesitate. "And I'm not just saying that because I don't particularly enjoy dragging Rusty to the bathroom."

They released Rusty, and he shot out of the bathtub and into the kitchen.

Madeline followed him to give the promised treat. "But you know about my ex-husband and how he betrayed me."

Arianna scoffed behind her. "Brandon is nothing like your ex. He's one of the good ones. Your ex… If Jessie hadn't arrested him, I would've been tempted to put a bullet in him."

"Thanks. I think." Impressed and just a little scared, Madeline handed Rusty the treat, which he jumped to get. Then she refreshed his water bowl, added kibble to his other bowl, and washed her hands. "I can cook something for lunch, but…" Her heart stuttered. "It reminds me of cooking with Brandon."

Arianna rolled her eyes as she poured herself a glass of mango juice. "At this point, *breathing* would remind you of him."

Not a pleasant discovery, was it? Madeline took out a water bottle from the fridge, the smooth surface cold against her fingers.

Arianna lifted her glass in a silent toast. "It's okay about lunch. I'm sure Genevieve will cook up a storm. She always does. If you're not going to call Brandon, you need a distraction. I don't want to see you sulking."

Maybe Arianna had been right the first time. Shopping could cheer Madeline up. If she shopped for gifts for her girls, it would also give her a chance to see Jessie for lunch in Springfield. So after a quick phone call to Jessie, Madeline picked up her purse from her room and told Rusty to be good.

"I'm going to Springfield. Do you need anything?"

Arianna walked into the hall, her nose in her laptop. She must be doing one of those mysterious assignments. "No. I should go with you, though."

Madeline's curiosity was piqued, but she didn't ask. She had too much unknown in her own life to start poking into others. "No, you're busy. It's okay. Jessie will meet me for lunch and shopping. I'll be fine."

She lifted her chin. It was time to be assertive again. She didn't need a babysitter. Including Brandon.

Arianna looked up and tilted her head as if she wasn't so sure about the fine part. "Pay attention to your surroundings. Call me if you see anything suspicious. Anything at all. Or even better, call Brandon. Do you have your gun?"

Madeline grimaced. "Why would I need...? Okay. Never mind." She returned to her bedroom and unlocked the safe. Then she removed a small caliber gun nestled among her velvet jewelry boxes—none of which were the engagement ring she wished for.

She winced. What a ridiculous thought. They weren't even dating. So why did longing for him slam into her with the same force she slammed the safe door?

On the way to Springfield, she turned on the radio, then turned it off. It was a country station, and Brandon liked country songs. She stared at the horses along the side of the road, then passed a rusty truck and cringed. Arianna had a point. Everything, every breath, every beat of her own heart reminded her of him now.

He was that huge a part of her world. He was that huge a part of her.

Jessie helped her forget about him for a bit, but on the way back, memories of him returned.

Madeline took a deep breath of lavender-scented car air freshener, which should be comforting. After all, it was her favorite scent. But she wished it smelled like leather and hay. Somehow, Brandon's scent became way more comforting.

How had she gotten so attached? When she'd been told that all her life she'd done her best to assert her independence, sometimes too much? She tightened her grip on the steering wheel and concentrated on the road. But it wasn't enough. She needed something else to concentrate on.

In her mind, she went over the photos on her laptop, phone, and social media. She'd seen plenty of photos with her foster sisters and even more of Rusty, and those had her smiling. But on social media, she rarely posted photos with her friends, presumably to give them privacy. Considering Jessie's and Arianna's professions, they needed that low profile. The same went for Paisley because of her secret project.

Most of the photos Madeline posted on her social media were of herself in glamorous dresses at charitable galas and prestigious social events. Some of them were with her then-husband, and they had, indeed, made a stunning pair. Too bad his character hadn't matched his dashing appearance.

When the snapshots were of her in the crowd, a lot of glances were on her. She'd been pleased at first.

But after speaking with Jenna, Madeline realized that, just like her family photos, those glamorous photos only depicted a glossy illusion of happiness.

Maybe the beautiful dresses and shoes were a defense mechanism, together with the confidence she'd tried to project, the confidence a lot of people might've taken for arrogance. Traumatized as a child, she'd hidden behind such things and a steely attitude like a medieval knight hid behind armor. After all, cutting herself could only go so far and eventually had to stop.

There were photos of her spectacular former house, and posting them was a mistake. No wonder she'd gotten robbed. All those antique vases, expensive paintings, and glittery chandeliers shouldn't have been displayed, and most likely Jessie had told her as much. But a part of Madeline understood her need to project outward success. With her good taste and eye for art, she'd decorated the house beautifully. But just like her dresses and jewelry, it was her armor to hide her pain. Maybe she intended part of it to impress people, too. She wanted to be liked, probably as much as her ex had wanted to make a career in local politics, and looking good and giving lavish parties at a nice home had seemed an easy way to accomplish that.

She slowed around a curve and searched for regret. No, she didn't regret letting the house go and wouldn't have regretted it even if a tragedy hadn't happened there. Living in such a huge place by herself—well, her and Rusty—would've been lonely. Her Realtor had sold it to a large family, for which Madeline was grateful.

She'd read those comments on her social media posts of glitz and glamor. Lots were admiring. But not all. Was it envy?

Or did people understand she'd been playing pretend, covering what was missing inside with outside beauty and success? She didn't have the word for it yet, but Brandon had shown her what was missing. Now, she didn't want to let it go.

Didn't want to let him go.

Her eyes narrowed as a car passed her. She was supposed to watch for a tail. She forgot, of course. She was off-balance, thrown even more off after Brandon revealed their breakup. She didn't know how to be on guard and didn't want to.

But there was more to it than the aching need to feel safe and protected again, the way she'd felt with Brandon. Jessie and Arianna would step up to protect her if she allowed them. While Jessie was a professional at that, Arianna also had skills that almost scared Madeline sometimes.

Madeline sped up and passed two cars to make it easier to figure out whether she had a tail.

With all her confidence on the outside, she wasn't that confident on the inside. Her security blanket had been stripped off when she'd been little, and she'd been thrown into the world shivering in many senses, helpless and defenseless.

The illusion of someone beautiful, confident, and later successful was her way to survive. She knew it now. If Genevieve had obtained admiration by caring about people and, well, feeding them, if Paisley had attracted people by her sunshine attitude, Madeline had gone an easier route. She already had an attractive appearance. She'd just needed to enhance it.

Maybe she'd persuaded herself that what others had thought of her didn't matter to her, but that was another illusion. Instead, it had mattered too much.

Had she switched her profession choice from a physician to a medical examiner partly because always appearing perfect began to exhaust her? Unlike her foster sisters, she'd found communicating with people outside their small circle difficult. So she'd chosen the route where she wouldn't have to work with live people.

Oh, why couldn't she have inherited her mother's sociable character? Instead, Madeline seemed to be even less sociable than her father.

For some time, she'd constructed the illusion of a good life so efficiently she'd almost believed it herself. She had a handsome and rich husband and an expensive house where she'd forced herself to give elegant parties. Her husband, planning to run for public office, had been even better than she was at creating illusions of great appearances.

She remembered it now as more memories rushed in.

The parties had been tiring and not her forte, but all they'd required from her was a constant polite smile and a beautiful appearance. Her ex hadn't even allowed her to cook for their guests, saying her skills weren't good enough. Deep inside, she'd understood she was just another decoration, a slight upgrade from a marble statue. But she needed that part of the illusion to help her forget her childhood nightmares. Forget she'd failed to save the people she loved the most.

Was she happy? No. But society thought she was happy and admired her, and that was something.

Everyone had the need to be admired, to be noticed, to be known. Not to be a failure and a disappointment. Maybe people who'd grown up with parents had that need satisfied somewhat. She'd lacked that, and the need had gone deep under her skin, like razors had gone under her skin in her younger years.

She probably hadn't thought much about it before because she had neither the time nor the desire.

Then her husband's betrayal and Jessie driving through the floor-to-ceiling window had shattered her house of glass. When she'd looked in the mirror for the first time after she'd been rescued, she didn't see the confident, flawless woman she'd tried so hard to project, especially after getting married. Trembling and cold, she saw a frightened girl again.

Then she'd done her best to slip back into her familiar armor. But it wasn't working any longer. She'd come to Cowboy Crossing to help her foster sisters, but she'd stayed because she couldn't return to the life she knew. She was still lost, though in a different way now. Maybe she'd needed to look at the world through the eyes of that scared girl to realize what had happened, to accept it, and to move on—finally.

Avoiding it all her life hadn't worked so well, had it?

Ironically, before she'd lost her memories, she'd avoided or suppressed many of them. Amnesia and learning everything about herself anew had made her examine her life and herself.

What had that left her?

While Jenna searched for clues in the outside world, Madeline needed to search within herself, and not just for clues.

She'd looked for love and validation from others when she should've looked inside herself. While she'd always liked the way she looked and had done her best to appear attractive, she wasn't sure her soul matched her looks. A lot of people who knew her would be shocked to hear it, but she didn't particularly like the person she was. Being friendly and picking up on social cues wasn't easy for her, and her gloomy mood had become a far more familiar companion than a cheerful one.

Yes, guys in high school and later the men she'd met had sought out her attention because she was a challenge, and it was sort of a competition who'd get her. But she'd never wanted to be a trophy.

Was that another reason she'd walked away from people? Had she been afraid they'd discover her beauty was only skin deep, she was shallow? Or was it because she couldn't show them her weak spots? She'd barely survived being hurt as a child. She'd learned to protect those spots.

She took a deep breath of lavender-scented car air freshener. It was time to change all that. It was time to seek validation from within. It was time to treat that scared child inside her with kindness instead of pushing her away. It was time to determine herself worthy of love, first and foremost her own.

And it was time to stop caring about what others thought of her. To stop hiding her vulnerabilities.

Because that had been the reason she'd broken up with Brandon. He'd seen her at a low point in life when her wrist had been broken and her heart crushed. He'd seen her vulnerability, as little as she'd allowed him to see, but still. Even if she knew he wouldn't use it to hurt her, her habit was to put up immediate walls. To shut him out.

Maybe it wouldn't have worked between them anyway then. She'd needed to learn that being weak, vulnerable, and open to others was okay, that, even in such a state, she was worthy of love. Maybe *especially* in such a state.

She'd needed to accept all sides of herself, not only the ones that were, well, perfect.

The deep longing for Brandon was more than a desire to feel admired and cherished, though there was that. She could return to Houston and call up her former suitors or find new ones. But only the admiration of one man mattered now. Because only one man mattered now. She wanted Brandon back, desperately. She missed his family, especially his mother who'd accepted her as if she were her own daughter. She even missed the horses, especially the foal. But selfishly, most of all, she missed the giddiness and budding happiness.

Not driving to his family ranch took all her willpower.

She was close to Cowboy Crossing when she noticed the tail. Her heart tumbled to her brake pedal.

What to do?

Chapter Fourteen

BRANDON'S HEART STUTTERED at Madeline's name on the phone screen. He'd hoped she'd call but didn't want it to be false hope.

With his palms clammy, the phone slipped to the floor. Of all days, he'd chosen this one to catch up on paperwork and sales orders in his cramped office.

Gnashing his teeth, he picked up the phone.

Please don't be broken. Please don't be broken.

Air whooshed out of his lungs. The phone was still ringing, and the screen seemed intact. He swiped to answer it. "Madeline!" Even doing his best to sound nonchalant, he couldn't keep the joy out of his voice. He'd never been as great at hiding his emotions as she was.

But only long beeps were his answer.

Argh.

He called her back. Would she answer? Or would she change her mind about talking to him?

"Brandon, I need your help." Her voice was tight, scared.

Right. Why else would she call him? Not because she missed him as much as he missed her. Or because she wanted to get back together.

But she'd come to him, hadn't she? He'd take what he could, but he wasn't the most patient man in the world. "What can I help you with?" He logged out of his laptop to give her his full attention.

The pause sent an unpleasant jolt in his gut. "It might be nothing, but... I think I'm being followed."

His heart dropped to the floor where his phone had recently been. Everything in him went on high alert, and he bolted to his feet. "Where are you now?" He snatched his keys, then removed his gun from the safe, and jammed it in the holster on his belt.

"About ten minutes from Cowboy Crossing. I think. Maybe less." The motor's growl in the background increased as if she pressed on the gas pedal.

He was already out the office door that he didn't bother to lock and sprinting to his truck. "Drive to my place at the ranch. I'll meet you halfway."

"No. I don't want to bring danger to your door."

Did that mean she cared about him? He revved the engine and took off, peeling rubber. "You can't bring it to your foster sisters, either." That must be why she'd called him instead of driving there. Even if the lodge had fences, bulletproof doors, and a security alarm, some risk remained.

"I know." She huffed, her voice miserable.

Something tender squeezed his heart. "I have five brothers, and three of them are here. We all have firearms and know how to use them. Plus, there are the cowhands."

"What about your parents? I can't put them at risk."

He suppressed a groan as he floored the gas pedal. She had him there.

"How about a public place? Somewhere my brothers and I can meet you? The park, for example?" He grimaced, realizing his faux pas. The place was traumatic for her. "Or not."

"Okay, that sounds like a compromise I can live with."

He forced a deep breath as his chest tightened further—although this time, a hard, cold band gripped it, not tenderness. "Just... be careful.... Please."

"I will. I have a gun with me. Arianna insisted. I just don't like to use it."

As her voice trembled, he wanted to reach out through the distance and hug her and hold her. She disconnected, and he had to let go of even her voice.

All his senses on high alert, he called his brothers on the way. Life on the ranch was always busy, but they'd drop everything and show up. It was never discussed but had always been this way.

He made it to the park first and got out of the truck. Was he a sitting duck here? He frowned but refused to get back into the truck's relative safety. Two of his brothers showed up and joined him, their jaws tight, their eyes determined. They didn't say a word. Neither did they draw their weapons, but their jackets hung open, showing gun holsters and allowing easy access to their weapons. They positioned themselves so they could duck behind their vehicles if needed. Ronan was tied up in helping in a shoplifting incident but would be here as soon as he could, probably with lights flashing.

Brandon's heartbeat ticked away painful seconds until her flashy car revved around the corner. He glanced at Kieran and Sean who gave him a curt nod. A quiet understanding passed between them.

A navy-blue SUV hung close behind her, but when she slid into the parking lot, the SUV moved along. He zeroed in on the license plate but only caught the first letters.

"Should we give chase?" Kieran asked.

Brandon waited a moment, just in case she'd meant a different car, but nothing showed up, so he nodded. He needed to stay with Madeline.

His brothers' trucks disappeared while he rushed to her luxury car. She slipped out, pale and wide-eyed. But her shoulders were drawn back, and she wasn't as shaken as he'd expected.

Unsure, he opened his arms. His chest swelled when she stepped into them.

"Thank you for showing up," she whispered over the rustle of wind in the leaves. "I wasn't nice to you lately or... or for a while, apparently. And still, you showed up."

"Of course, I did. I'll always show up for you." Wasn't that the truth.

As much as he enjoyed having her in his arms again, he couldn't take advantage of her vulnerable moment. Besides, it might not be safe to stand like this out in the open. He did his best to be aware of his surroundings, but his gaze kept returning to her.

Reluctantly, he let her go. But then he couldn't resist. He cupped her beautiful face and looked her in the eyes. "I know our relationship is on shaky ground right now. But stay with me this evening, please. I'll keep you safe." He might not be able to keep his heart safe at the same time, but he'd take that risk.

Her eyelashes fluttered, not in a coquettish way but like the fragile wings of a wounded bird. "I can't make any promises."

"I'm not asking for any." He stepped back, giving her the space she'd asked for.

"That's unfair to you." Regret dimmed her eyes. For the past? For the future? For the possibility she might hurt him again? Then her delectable mouth tipped up. "Do you have cocoa and marshmallows at your place?"

He nodded to both the marshmallows and to the fact that it was unfair to him. She was getting back into her car, saying she'd follow him. That was what mattered.

Keeping her alive and well.

They made it to his place without any adventures. He gestured for her to stay in the car while he did a quick check of what his cop brother called an outer perimeter.

Kieran called him as Brandon and Madeline rushed to the house. "Sorry, bro. We lost the SUV."

Brandon didn't let his disappointment affect his voice. "It's okay. Thanks for your help." He disconnected, resolving to talk to Ronan later.

Then Brandon opened the door for her.

What would she think of his small ranch house? His heart shifted as he unlocked the massive front door.

He shouldn't have checked her social media. Now he couldn't shed the photos of the house she used to live in. A mansion fit for royalty.

Unlike that place, his had no chandeliers or expensive paintings. Okay, there were paintings, but they weren't expensive. Free, actually, if not to count materials and labor.

He'd never thought much about it. When he'd caught up with the paperwork and everyone's pay and duties, he spent time with animals and vice versa. Recently, the young woman who'd cooked for the ranch hands since his mother stepped back had left for Springfield, so he'd stepped up to help cook before a new one was hired. Then he ate with the other cowhands. In whatever spare time he had left, he helped with the troubled teens. Home was a place to shower and sleep, not much else. Except for painting in his studio on some Sundays.

But now he cringed, wishing he'd put more thought into his décor. Inviting her here wasn't his best idea. But the vulnerability in her stunning blue eyes distracted him, and he'd wanted to get her someplace safe—fast. It was too late to change that now.

He stepped inside after her and ground his molars.

Traces of mud smeared the hardwood floor near the entrance, and cowboy boots, caked in mud as well, slumped nearby. He should've thrown his worn-out jacket into the laundry instead of on the back of the chair. The leather sofa and armchairs were okay, but the rug depicting horses was thin from wear.

At least, he'd kept the place relatively uncluttered, mostly because he hadn't bothered to buy much furniture except for a few sturdy wooden pieces. It was also a plus that he rarely ate at home, so no dishes or leftover food cluttered the pristine kitchen.

But the place wasn't anywhere close to her standards. Her mouth opened as she looked around. Oh no. Was she that disappointed?

His fingers twitched to mess with his ridiculous haircut, to fix *something* to her standards. But he clenched them at his sides. He was who he was. And he'd grow his hair back out the way he liked it to prove it.

"Wow. This is amazing." She stepped forward.

He could use several adjectives to describe his home, but amazing wasn't one of them. He cleared his throat, hoping she wasn't being sarcastic. "What exactly is amazing?"

"The painting." She approached the Western painting nearly taking up the living room's entire south wall. Then she glanced back. "May I see more of your paintings, if you have them?"

He shifted from one leg to the other. Was that a good idea? He'd self-consciously regretted opening his home to her, but his studio was far more personal. His mouth went dry.

"Yes." He gestured for her to follow.

This was his favorite room. North facing, it had large windows looking out to the lawn. They bathed the fresh-canvas-white walls and blank-sheet tile floors with light on most days. He could forget everything and lose himself in the beauty of nature and art.

Well, he couldn't forget *everything*.

Her eyes widened. "How... how many paintings of me do you have?"

"I haven't counted."

Maybe keeping a part of her when she'd walked away wasn't right. Something was twisted about it. He'd gotten to keep a part of her without her permission because she'd never posed for the portraits. But they'd helped him cope.

She walked along the row of her portraits, her eyes turning sad. "You see me better than I am."

"That's impossible."

She was aware of her good looks. She'd been a model, after all, and later had dressed to attract attention—and keep it. So what had she meant?

He turned back to the paintings. He'd tried to capture her enigmatic smile, the way her face lit up in the rare moments of laughter. That was the way he'd wanted to remember her.

That was the way he'd wanted her to be.

"You see me happy," she whispered.

"That's because I want you happy."

She chuckled without mirth. "That's a tall order."

He stepped closer and shoved his hands into his pockets to avoid touching her. Her signature lavender scent mixed with the aroma of oil and wood. "What would it take for you to be happy?"

She opened her mouth as if about to reply, then shook her head. Glossy hair slipped over her shoulders, falling along her face, shielding her as she averted her gaze.

Now, his fingers twitched to sweep it aside, to sweep aside everything blocking her heart and soul from him.

But he dared not. He'd had everything he needed for happiness right where he was born. As the burning ache inside him increased, he realized maybe not everything. But while he could try to capture her image on canvas, he couldn't keep her in his world.

Maybe like a wounded bird, she'd stayed in Cowboy Crossing to recover from her past and would fly away as soon as she could.

He wanted her to recover. He'd meant what he'd said. He wanted her to be happy. Even if it meant he'd have to lose her again.

She flicked her hair back, raising her chin. "I can be sulky. I'm distant with people, but it's mostly because I don't know how to express myself with them." Her lips wobbled before she ducked her head again. "I guess I'm afraid that, once they know the real me, they'll be disappointed my personality doesn't match my looks."

Could beautiful Madeline, who projected so much confidence some people in Cowboy Crossing considered her arrogant, be so self-conscious? Even insecure?

He'd thought they'd come from different worlds, but maybe they weren't so different, after all. She wasn't just the gorgeous image from a glossy magazine page. She was a real person with doubts, faults, and hurts. Way more hurts than he'd realized, though he'd sensed some of them.

It was as if she were afraid that, if she showed her weaknesses, she'd disappoint people.

He stepped to her, let his fingers slip around the hair falling into her face, and eased it aside. "I don't know how to express myself with people, either. That's why I love working with animals and paint. How about expressing yourself with art like I do?"

She snorted, and the sound that would be unladylike coming from someone else sounded lovely coming from her. "I tried to draw as a child. I could only draw stick figures. While I love collecting art, I'm useless at creating it."

He placed his hands on her forearms, partly unable to resist the draw of her flowery scent, the draw of her smooth skin, and partly to emphasize his words to persuade her. "That's fine. Canvas will never judge or be disappointed in you. Neither will I."

Emotion filled her eyes, but she didn't shift away. "Even if I eventually leave?"

His heart sank to the tiled floor. "Okay, I'd be disappointed then."

Disappointed? Try, heartbroken again. Much worse than the first time.

Because the first time he'd fallen for the woman he'd thought she could be, still learning to accept her. Now he was falling for the person she truly was, with way more dimensions than he'd realized.

His arms fell to the sides, and disappointment seemed to flash in her blue eyes before vanishing, leaving too soon to be sure. He'd never hidden his emotions, but she seemed to be a pro. While he'd discovered it was her defense mechanism, why did she need those defenses with him?

A thought wormed in. Hadn't she told him? She was afraid to disappoint people. Could that have included him?

He didn't ask because she'd already stepped aside and stood studying the blank canvas. The tender moment between them evaporated with the oily scent of paints.

She stilled near the canvas like a bird unsure whether to take flight or stay and try to get the worm.

"That's the beauty of the blank canvas. You can paint whatever you want on it. Even if it's a black square, which by the way became famous and started a new art movement." He opened the box with paintbrushes and gave her the choice.

She hesitated. "Like the beauty of starting life with a blank slate…" She'd seemed to love it at first, showing a more cheerful side until all the doubts crept in.

"Yes." She reached for the medium-size paintbrush. "But I'm not a blank slate. I'm the way I am. I'll never be constantly cheerful like Paisley or warm and caring like Genevieve."

"I wouldn't expect you to change." A thought needled. Didn't he like the new sides of Madeline a little too much?

His doubt reflected in her eyes, but once again, she deflected by turning away.

Talking about paints would be a safer topic. He reached for the palette and tubes. "What colors would you like to use?"

She pulled up her hair and pinned it at her nape, presumably to stop it from being streaked with paint. "Blue."

Right. He should've guessed. He opened the tubes and mixed several shades of blue, then eyed the elegant teal-hued dress now hugging her as he ached to. "Um, you won't want to get that dress dirty." He thought of offering her his apron and a cap. Or would that be beneath her? Here he was, stereotyping her again.

"It's okay," she said, making his eyes widen. "Okay, I'm not going to paint horses because I wouldn't want to offend them. Or you, for the same reason." She dipped her brush into aquamarine.

He chuckled. "I wouldn't get offended."

She gave him a pointed look. "You don't know how bad my painting skills are."

And if she was bad at something, she didn't do it. He guessed that much. She stared at the white surface with an upraised brush.

He understood it. A blank canvas, while alluring, could be intimidating. Just like starting anew. "I have an idea. How about I guide your hand? We'll paint the sky."

She nodded, and he wrapped his fingers around hers.

Moments later, it didn't seem like such a sensible idea. Her proximity wreaked havoc on his senses, sending his heart beating wildly against his rib cage. As his breathing went shallow, he took some satisfaction in the fact that hers went faster, as well.

Excitement and apprehension mixed with awareness, different emotions swirling and blending into each other like different hues of blue paint. He should be looking at the canvas, but his gaze kept returning to the exposed line of her graceful neck.

Attraction surged in his veins, flooding them like rivers after too much rain. A man could have only so much willpower. Gathering whatever was left of his self-control, he managed to do a few brushstrokes. Right now, his mind was way cloudier than the canvas sky.

Usually, working on paintings relaxed him, but this time, his erratic pulse accelerated. He shouldn't take advantage of having her so close. He really shouldn't. But he caressed her fingers, sending a jolt to his heart.

Then she leaned into him, so trusting, and it was his undoing. He couldn't move. Wasn't even sure he should be breathing.

After a few blissful moments, she said, "This isn't going to work."

She'd better mean them painting together and not their relationship.

Neither one of them moved. Then she guided his hand and placed the brush on the palette. But she didn't step away. So he wrapped his arms around her, breathing her in and holding her in.

He ached for her to stay, not just as a beautiful image in his studio. But for now, he'd create a precious memory of having her in his arms. And maybe she was doing the same.

After a while, she said, "I should go."

Despite her words, she didn't move.

Thankful for that, he made another attempt. "How about we finger paint?"

She eased out of his embrace and turned around to face him. "Finger paint? Like children, dipping our hands in paint and pressing on the surface?"

"Yes." He nodded.

Of course, that could get messy, and Madeline didn't do messy. On the other hand, she'd worked at the stables, and while he'd kept them clean, they weren't exactly a sparkling palace.

The corners of her mouth lifted, but he couldn't allow his attention to linger on her mouth, or he'd kiss her senseless.

"Okay," she said.

"Okay?" he parroted.

"Okay."

He'd said he wasn't a great conversationalist, but he shouldn't be proving it this much.

He could imagine Madeline as a child, laughing and playing in the mud in the years before tragedy and sadness crept into the broken crevices of her soul. He craved to bring that joy back even more than he craved to kiss her, and that was saying something.

Then he eyed her fancy dress again. He was about to ask her about it when she placed her palm into the paint mixture and then pressed it to the canvas. She did that three times, tilted her head, and gestured to him. "Your turn."

Not something he'd intended to do, but all right. Her handprint looked so delicate, her fingers long and slender, near his large palm. His heart squeezed from the need to protect her, mostly from herself. And then they still didn't know who'd attacked her in the park and whether it was connected with the murder of her parents. Or where Matt Luettgen, the man who'd threatened to harm her, was now.

But after learning more of her story, Brandon knew better than to consider her a fragile figurine, ready to slip off and shatter. She was a survivor, and she had a steel spine.

She walked backward, probably to see their "hand" handiwork from another perspective. Sometimes he could see the whole picture from a distance better, too. Then she stumbled on the stool he'd foolishly left in the way.

"Madeline!" He bolted toward her as her arms flailed, reminding him of a bird again. He caught her in his arms. "I've got you."

Not that... that he had her. He didn't know whether she'd ever let anyone into her heart again. But for now, he was grateful not to let her fall.

Then it registered. He frowned at the paint stains his palms left on her dress. "Sorry. Let me help you with that." Paint stains were difficult to get out of fabric, and he usually painted in the clothes that, well, already had paint stains, so a few more wouldn't hurt.

She shrugged. "It's okay. Don't worry about it. It's just a dress."

Huh. "You're fine with not looking magazine-cover perfect? Though you're always perfect to me."

"Perfect?" She shook her head. "You have no idea how flawed I am."

"The flaws are what make you perfect. They are the best part." He wanted to cup her face but resisted for several reasons. First, it wasn't what friends did. Second, he didn't want to leave paint streaks on her face, too. She'd still look gorgeous, of course.

She reached toward him, then stared at the stains she created on his shirt. "Oops."

"Payback, right?" He grinned to show her he didn't mind.

She laughed, music to his ears. "No, that wasn't on purpose. You know what? I had a great time today."

"I had a great time, too." His heart warmed at the light in her eyes.

The pull toward her was so strong he couldn't resist any longer. Still, he didn't want to do something she wouldn't want him to. But before he could even ask, she wrapped her hands around his neck as if she couldn't resist the attraction, either. He didn't care if she left paint stains on his skin.

Anticipation pulled in his belly, swirling and growing. He dipped his head, and she met him halfway.

His every cell sang in delight as his lips brushed against hers. She stilled, and he did, as well, afraid she'd step away. But she deepened the kiss instead, and bright colors erupted in his mind. She tasted of promises and happiness, and he ached for it to last forever, even if he knew it couldn't.

If she left, he was going to miss that laugh, as rare as it was. He was going to miss her with a passion.

In fact, though she was still here, he already missed her with his entire being.

Chapter Fifteen

MADELINE DID HER BEST to persuade herself this was just a friendly dinner between friends at a local barbecue restaurant and their amazing kiss was just a one-time mistake that shouldn't have happened. But with her pulse rapid, her whole heart ached for this to be a date.

She'd never say it out loud, though. Brandon pulled the chair out for her, and she sat. She shivered, too self-conscious of his fleeting touch on the small of her back, his attentive gaze, his signature scent of hay and leather with a touch of musk—a scent now bringing her back to their time together and the kiss that still made her insides tingle. The kiss she longed to experience again so much it scared her.

She fiddled with her napkin, her mind as restless as her fingers. She didn't understand what was happening inside her. On one hand, she longed for his touch and his attention. On the other hand, that resistance balked against letting him too close. She wished she could explain it by him fibbing to her, but she suspected it was much deeper.

Her feelings were almost as much a mystery as her memories. Or maybe they all entwined together.

All she knew was her bones went soft when he as much as looked at her. When he'd kissed her, she'd gone liquid and couldn't remember the reasons she needed to keep her distance.

"They have a karaoke night on Fridays. So, um, today," he said. Neither of them had brought up the kiss. Probably for the better.

She latched onto the distraction of the karaoke thing.

Right. Like she'd ever go to the makeshift stage and sing. With her voice, that would be embarrassing. She'd never had musical talent, and her singing was even worse than her drawing. Arianna had self-taught herself to play the guitar in high school, but Madeline couldn't even learn simple chords.

She'd once sang "Happy Birthday" with other people at her then-husband's party, and he'd scolded her so much afterward she'd resolved never to sing in public again. Argh, couldn't her memory bring her something more pleasant?

Singing karaoke here would be embarrassing. And Madeline didn't do embarrassing. Her cheeks flamed up. She'd had enough public humiliation when she'd gone from half of the golden couple, admired by many, to a heartbroken and betrayed divorcée, pitied by most.

Hold on.

Did she remember that, too?

Her memories didn't appear as a flood of images, and she still couldn't recall anything after she'd arrived in Cowboy Crossing. But the times before had arrived in bits and pieces. Like the memory of dancing with her then-husband at a charity gala, the music soft, his steps light, his smile dashing, but that smile hadn't reached his eyes when he gave it to her.

Then a shudder passed through her as if she were still lying on the cold tile floor, tied and gagged, her limbs going numb, her mind panicking, her blood and fear clogging her nostrils. *Here we go again.*

Why couldn't she recall something good instead?

"Are you okay?" Brandon reached out to her, bringing her to the present where enticing scents of barbecue floated around them. Spring wildflowers graced the rustic table, and ranch gear decorated the barnwood walls. A young girl sang a love ballad near the karaoke machine and did a good job of it, her clear voice rising to the open ceiling beams.

Madeline took a deep breath. She was safe here with him. Comforted. She wasn't on that cold tile floor. She stared at his fingers on her forearm, pleasant tingles spreading through her and warming her inside. Maybe she could make new, much happier memories.

Because they would involve him.

Unlike her and her ex, Brandon had never been about appearances. He was all substance.

He removed his hand way too fast, and she missed it.

Why had she broken up with him, despite her obvious attraction and growing feelings and all his great qualities? She couldn't understand it, but it must've been something important.

Maybe that was why she'd tried to steel herself against this overwhelming attraction. She needed to know why she'd walked away because, so far, she couldn't find a fault with him.

Of course, he wasn't perfect and could be grouchy sometimes, but that was part of the attraction.

Or did she walk away not because there was something wrong with him but because there was something wrong with *her*? The attachment issues she and her foster sisters all seemed to have, though some more than others? What a sobering thought.

And what about the possibility of her return to Houston? It wasn't like she could be a medical examiner in a small town. She couldn't ask him to go with her. It wouldn't be fair to him. He loved his ranch and his family and was a cowboy through and through.

Her heart squeezed painfully, and she leaned forward.

Then the waitress showed up with menus. "What would you like to drink?"

Madeline shifted back and asked for lemonade while Brandon went for iced tea.

When he'd kissed her yesterday in the studio, attraction and excitement simmered under her skin. He had an undeniable ability not only to paint her beautiful but also to paint her world beautiful. But could she do the same for him? She had too much hurt inside her, too much unknown, too much turmoil—and it scared her.

She placed the menu aside. She already knew she'd get chicken wings, just like the previous time. Only now, she didn't have the giddiness of starting anew. She knew herself better now. He'd liked the cheerful Madeline. But that wasn't the real Madeline.

As she breathed in the hearty scents of hamburgers and onion rings from a neighboring table, her stomach rumbled in anticipation of chicken wings. He'd taught her to enjoy simple, real things in life instead of constantly building an illusion, and she smiled her gratitude. She looked forward to seeing the little foal again, to spending time with the horses, to finger painting, especially if it involved being in his arms again. Her heartbeat sped up just at the thought.

But what could she offer him in return except for heartbreak? He had a passion for helping people and animals, which she admired. But was she just a project to him? Both when he'd met her and then after her amnesia she'd been at low points in her life, not exactly helpless, but close. She'd initially thought her beauty attracted him to her, but she knew better now. Could it be her weakness instead?

The menu slipped from her hands and fell onto the table, and her gut tightened.

The waitress returned with the drinks, and they placed their orders. He went for a cheeseburger. The young girl with blue lips and black fingernails disappeared with their menus and orders, and Madeline's attention switched back to Brandon.

Their gazes met and held, and the room temperature seemingly kicked up a notch. Her body leaned toward him before she could stop it, and she longed for his touch and kiss again. She'd asked him just to be friends, and he'd agreed. Then she'd failed spectacularly. She was too far gone, too deeply attracted to him just to be friends.

Looking at him meant she'd be lost in his brown eyes and wouldn't remember all the reasons she should resist.

So she reached for the smooth, cold glass and a more neutral topic—or at least a scarier one. "I read through the files Jenna gathered for me." She took a hurried sip of cold, tangy liquid before proceeding to the part that bothered her. "I looked at the photos."

She studied a small scratch on the table. Barely noticeable. But it was there. She placed the glass on the table and touched the tiny groove with a fingertip.

When she looked up, his eyes searched hers. But he didn't say anything, and she was grateful for the latter.

The waitress brought their food and left, but neither Brandon nor Madeline moved.

She'd thought she'd inherited her mother's beauty and her father's personality, but after learning about the family secret, she wasn't so sure. She'd thought once she regained her memories she'd be on solid ground, know where she stood. Instead, she'd been caught in an earthquake with the ground still shaking because she couldn't even be certain who her father was.

The memories of her childhood when her parents had been alive, the ones she'd considered her happy times, the solid foundation of her character... The ones she'd cherished so much... Were some of them an illusion, as well? Was her life in some way an illusion, as well?

Oh, just say it. "I tried to figure out if I might look like..."

"Nonsense." Compassion flashed in his eyes. "You're slim and tall like your father. You have his intelligence for studies and talent for medicine. You have blue eyes like him, his hair color."

Wow. He'd paid attention to the family photos she'd hung on the lodge walls.

She reached for a chicken wing absentmindedly. "But not his blood type."

He stilled. "What?"

"I decided to look into it now. I'm type O negative. He's type AB." She dipped the chicken wing into ranch sauce and ate it without sensing its taste. Maybe she should've ordered a salad, after all. "I asked Jenna to talk to Salotto, my mother's former boyfriend, the one she'd had a longtime affair with. I don't know how Jenna managed to get him to volunteer this information, but he's type O negative."

Her blood type. She didn't say it, but she didn't need to. Maybe she shouldn't have started this conversation at dinner. She gestured to his abandoned cheeseburger. "Please eat."

He took the cheeseburger, then put it down. "That doesn't prove anything."

"But a DNA test will." If she could get Salotto to agree to it. If he refused, would she have the guts to pay him a visit in Houston, excuse herself to use the bathroom, and steal his toothbrush?

She grimaced. She wasn't proud of that thought, but she was tired of secrets. As soon as she figured out or remembered something, new mysteries showed up.

Brandon's hand moved toward her but then stopped. "I'm sorry."

She helped herself to another wing, wishing he did reach out to her. "Salotto had a motive. And if he and Mom used the lake house for their rendezvous, he'd know the alarm code. Would know about Dad and Mom's plans, too."

"But Salotto had an alibi." He started on his cheeseburger.

Good. She didn't want him to go hungry on her behalf. "So did the disgruntled relative of my dad's patient. At first." She reached for one of his fries, knowing he'd share.

But maybe Salotto wasn't the type of man to share. Especially if he'd found out Madeline was his daughter. But then why had he never contacted her, let her go into foster care?

Argh. Would she ever know? Even if she could build a life with Brandon, which was doubtful, she couldn't ask him to commit to a woman whose baggage towered higher than a skyscraper.

"I hope you'll get the closure you need." His fingers lingered over hers, then touched them briefly, and withdrew.

"Thank you." She wasn't hungry for chicken wings anymore, she was hungry for more of his touch, more of this physical connection that was real and not a vague mystery. But she couldn't allow herself to show that desperate need. She had to grow back the spine she'd shown so well before.

She needed more than closure. She needed Brandon. But that would be asking too much.

"I don't remember everything from my childhood yet. But there are some images with Dad. Him taking me to the park and me laughing on the swing. Him lifting me in the air when coming home. Then one day he became... more distant. I'd tried so hard to win back his attention, but I kept doing it wrong. Messing it up. Or so I thought. The only time he'd been tender with me was when I scratched my knees or pricked my fingers on thorns or some other thing. Then he'd turn his doctor mode on for me, which was better than ignoring me or scolding." Which might have been why she resorted to cutting herself later—or had she started hurting herself for attention even before he'd died? "Mom said he was too busy with his important work to spend time with us. But maybe..."

"He found out." Brandon said the words she didn't want to.

Something inside her broke once again. "Yes." She sighed. "It's all supposition, of course." She might never know the entire truth.

Would she be better off if she didn't know, didn't suspect all this?

Brandon cocked his head and narrowed his eyes. "Did you hear anything about Matt Luettgen?"

Grateful for the change of topic, she sank back in her seat, but this one wasn't much better. "Jessie talked to one of his buddies. Luettgen stopped at his place on the way to Springfield." She sighed again. "He was belligerent about how I ruined his life. He said I was going to pay for it."

Brandon's features hardened. "I'm not going to allow that."

How could he make that promise? Already, too many obligations tugged at him from different sides. He couldn't be with her all the time. "Thank you. But I'm not your responsibility. I do appreciate everything you've done for me. I'm sure others do, too. But... maybe you shouldn't overextend yourself."

He took a bite of his cheeseburger, but his posture shifted slightly back. "I do it for me, too. I like to be liked."

She rolled her eyes as she took another sip of her cold drink. "Don't you know it? People like you just the way you are." She did, for sure. "You don't have to earn it."

He didn't say anything. Helping others seemed to be the foundation of his life. Had she just tried to take a wrecking ball to it? The chicken wings soured in her stomach. She kept messing up relationships, just like she'd kept messing up getting her father's love back.

Something clicked in her mind. She'd just told Brandon he didn't need to earn anyone's love. But hadn't she tried to earn love? First with her parents. Because baking with her mother and helping her in the garden had earned her mother's approval. She'd done so many things to earn back her dad's approval, from getting his favorite flowers and bringing him the remote, to choosing a profession in the medical field. She'd done everything to earn her ex's approval.

She'd been told she didn't care what others thought of her. She'd projected that distant air. In reality, she'd cared too much.

It was a lot to process.

They ate in silence. Then she'd tried to channel her inner gratitude, a method not inherent but learned the hard way. She had a great man by her side, even if not for long, and great food. Being sulky wasn't the way to give thanks for it.

Her appetite returned, and her taste buds rejoiced. She stole his fries with more enthusiasm and offered him some wings. She didn't know what her future held. She didn't even know her past.

But she *knew* she wanted to enjoy her time with Brandon. He'd never looked at her as a trophy like many men had before but had cared about her even when she wasn't kind to him. People often compared her with a diamond—and gifted her diamonds, too—but he was the real diamond here.

Sharing the meal with him and seeing the attraction in his eyes was precious. Even breathing the same air with him was precious.

"I thought a lot about what you said in the studio," he finally said. "You say you're not warm and kind, but I beg to differ. I've seen the tender way you treat the horses and the little foal. When your friends needed you, you dropped everything to come and help. You adopted a rescue and volunteered at the animal shelter. My mom, who is a great judge of character, adores you."

His words warmed her, but he gave her too much credit. "That's because your mom is such a kind soul. And animals, especially little ones, are easy to love. As for my foster sisters, come on, you met them. How can anyone who experienced their care, a bit suffocating sometimes, not care about them in return? Jessie saved my life when my ex nearly got me killed. And Genevieve... Genevieve saved my life in a different way."

"True. But still, your coldness is your shield. You had to be on your own since being a child. You lost the people you loved at such a young age. Your world was turned upside down, and you never even had closure. So getting attached again, risking that kind of pain and uncertainty again, was scary."

She couldn't argue. It *was* traumatic. If that was right, could she ever allow people outside her small circle of foster sisters to be close to her again?

Again, just like in her portrait, he saw things in her she didn't allow anyone to see, even herself.

She tuned in to the songs.

A few people went to the karaoke machine, some better than others.

From the corner of her eye, she saw Arianna enter the restaurant, all dressed in black, as usual, and waved for her friend to join them. Arianna shook her head, pointing at the take-out box she'd just picked up. Then her gaze traveled to the karaoke machine. She stilled. Then she placed the box on the nearest vacant table and strode to the microphone.

As secluded as she was, she had the ability to transform in public. Like she did now. As soon as she took the first note, people stopped talking and even stopped eating, which was saying something with the awesome food.

While her voice entranced everyone, a few patrons started recording the performance on their phones. She didn't seem to have any jitters, didn't even look like she was aware of all the attention like Madeline would be. Instead, Arianna seemed lost in the song or in some faraway place. This wasn't a love song, but a song about being betrayed and hurt and surviving the pain to see another day.

Goose bumps erupted over Madeline's skin, and her throat closed. She wanted so badly to run to Arianna and wrap her in a hug and help her heal somehow. But as if feeling her thoughts, Arianna looked at her and shook her head almost imperceptibly.

When she finished, the applause was deafening. But she just replaced the microphone, picked up her take-out box, and took a seat.

Nobody went to the karaoke machine after that. Little surprise since even a good performer would pale in comparison.

Finally, Brandon got up. "I'm going to give it a try at the karaoke."

Madeline's eyes widened. "You can sing, too?" Seriously, how many talents did the man have?

He shrugged. "Not really."

She cleared her throat, not wanting him to embarrass himself. "Then do you really want to go sing after Arianna?" His expression changed, and Madeline gasped at her faux pas. "That didn't sound right."

He swallowed hard. "We have friendly people here."

And she should be one of those friendly people. She managed a smile. "If you'd like to sing, I'd love to hear it." It would've been better for his ego to do it in the privacy of the lodge, but she didn't add that. Besides, his ego must be much smaller than hers, and she'd do good to downsize hers.

He started the country song she liked on their drive to Springfield. She sent him an encouraging smile. Maybe he'd underestimated his singing abilities. He'd underestimated his artistic abilities and was humble in general.

A few moments passed. No, he hadn't underestimated them. Even with her lack of an ear for music, she could understand he missed most of the notes. His singing was truly awful. Her insides flamed up, twisting for him.

Arianna slipped onto a chair nearby. "Why don't you go join him?"

That was easy for Arianna to say.

"Are you kidding me?" Madeline's jaw slackened. "You know how bad my singing is. I don't even sing inside the house anymore because people might think someone is getting tortured!"

Arianna chuckled. Then her expression turned somber again. "Do you hear that song? It's a love song he's singing to you in the best way he can. The least you can do is support him."

"And share the embarrassment." Madeline's throat closed for a different reason.

Arianna knew Madeline was terrified of public humiliation. One of the reasons Madeline had done her best to look perfect in public. She didn't want to be a failure again.

Arianna shrugged. "That, too." Then her features softened. "Come on. I'll even go with you if you want me to."

It would be so easy to say yes.

But Arianna had a point. Madeline should support the man who'd supported her in everything he could. And despite how horrible his singing was, it still put a smile on her face. Just how bad could this be? Yet her insides tightened as she got up and hesitated. "Thanks, but I'll go by myself."

Arianna gave her an encouraging nod. "You can do this."

Madeline sometimes wished she could be like Paisley, who was quirky and unique and didn't care if she looked like a child who'd never grown up, pink dresses and butterfly headbands and all. Paisley was always herself, and that self was wonderful.

Well, what better time to start than now? Madeline walked to the microphone. The way Brandon's face lit up rewarded her, even if everything inside her trembled.

To her surprise, a healthy round of applause followed as the song ended, and she clapped in earnest, too. Nobody booed or showed their displeasure in any way. People were friendly here indeed.

That gave her courage.

She took the second microphone. "My name is Madeline, and I'm going to be a first-time singer here. Or anywhere, for that matter. Fair warning: my singing is going to be worse than Brandon's." That elicited a few chuckles. "So I hope I don't ruin your appetite."

"We're good here!" a few men shouted.

"She's a looker," someone said.

Well, she might be a looker, but a singer she was not.

Yet here we go.

Their duet exceeded her expectations. She'd imagined it was going to be bad, but it turned out much worse. Her cheeks flamed up, but then people cheered them on. Soon several others joined in, including Arianna, and by the end of the song, it was... well, rather tolerable.

It was a love song again, and as Brandon and Madeline sang the words and stared into each other's eyes, she could relate to the feelings of longing and passion. She might not be ready to think she was in love with Brandon, much less say it, but she was falling for him. For a few moments, the crowd disappeared, and she could only see the emotion in his brown eyes, the curve of his smile, the way he leaned toward her. And as reluctant as she'd been to join him on the makeshift stage, now she wanted the moment to linger.

A puzzling applause and more cheers resounded when they finished, and a pleasant wave washed through her.

She hugged Brandon and whispered in his ear, "Thank you. You did great."

"You, too."

With undeniable force, she ached for the words of love he'd been singing to come not from the text on the karaoke machine but from his heart. Even if she had no clue what she'd do if one day they did.

Chapter Sixteen

"BUT I CAN'T create art myself. How am I going to teach it?" Madeline blinked in surprise at Brandon's request over the phone the next day. "I doubt anyone wants lessons in finger painting."

Panic bubbled. She had no experience with children or teenagers—by choice, by the way. Didn't he know she wasn't a people person?

"You don't need to teach anything." His calming voice soothed her jitters. "Though frankly, you probably know more about art than I do. Please just stay with the class while I'm away. I need to go. It's an emergency. An animal is sick. I'll be back before the class is over."

Guilt stung her. He'd been pulled in so many directions, and he'd asked her a simple favor. But why did he try to help everyone in sight? Not only did he teach the teens to work with horses but he also held Saturday afternoon art classes for them? She grimaced as she glanced out of the lodge window. Didn't he understand he was just one person? Yes, hardworking and efficient, but one person.

He was also one person who mattered very much to her.

Then it registered. She should be grateful he'd called her with this request. And let's be honest, unlike many members of his family, she had time.

She could survive sticking around for a class. She'd gone to many parties and hosted many more for a man who wasn't worth it. She could manage a short art class for troubled teens for a man who was more than worth it.

"So I just need to be there? That's it?" she clarified.

"Often in life, that's all one needs to do," he said slowly. Then he added, "Well, in this case, make sure nobody is fighting or messing up the painting supplies. But they are pretty well-behaved in my class."

That didn't sound too reassuring.

"Right. I'll be there."

Apparently, it usually took her a while to get ready. But Brandon and his class were waiting for her, so she just stayed in the slacks and T-shirt she'd worn at home, swiped pink lipstick over her lips, and picked up her purse. She told Arianna and Genevieve, who were cooking in the kitchen, where she was going.

Both women gaped at her.

Arianna said, "That's the first time I've seen you going anywhere without elaborate makeup and in a T-shirt."

"I'm in a hurry." Madeline slipped her feet into the pumps she'd left near the door.

Arianna shrugged. "I used to think that, even if the house was on fire and you were in a hurry to get out, you'd still change into something fancy first and put on diamond jewelry."

Arianna was being sarcastic or... something, but the comment still stung as Madeline drove to the makeshift center for troubled teens. The gray brick building with large windows housed several offices and classrooms for courses and workshops. Since the place was close, she made it there in no time.

Soon about fifteen curious pairs of eyes stared as Brandon introduced her. Her skin crawled, but she plastered on a smile in a trained effort. She could do this.

Two pairs of those eyes were familiar. One set, cautious and guarded, belonged to Tommy, the boy who'd stolen her purse. She only glimpsed him before he hid behind the easel. Was he wearing the same jeans as at the parade? If so, they looked cleaner this time. His hair, still falling into his eyes, was combed, unlike that day. He sat at the end of the class as if he tried his best to stay unnoticed.

Another set, assessing but much warmer, belonged to the girl he'd liked. She was in the front row and close to the teacher's desk. Tommy had introduced her as Florence. Long, wavy, blonde hair reached her shoulders, and pale freckles spackled her delicate nose and high cheeks. She'd tucked a white T-shirt with cheery orange flowers into her pale jeans and used a set of gold-toned barrettes to keep her hair away from her face and paint splatter. Madeline had kept her promise and gifted the girl her purse—with a few other things in it like a new makeup kit—and baked her a cake.

Brandon leaned toward her and whispered, "Are you sure about this?"

Nope.

But she nodded and increased the wattage in her smile. "Absolutely."

Once he left, she perched on the wooden chair behind the desk, wishing she could hide behind an easel, too. She didn't know how to make small talk with adults, much less with teenagers. Her brows knitted, but she ironed out the frown, hopefully before anyone noticed. So far, nobody tried to paint each other instead of their canvases, and she was grateful.

After a few minutes, Florence eased her chair and easel closer to Madeline, and Madeline had already considered it too close for comfort. She tensed. She'd move her chair back, but she was close to the wall.

Florence leaned forward and whispered, "Is Mr. Brandon your boyfriend?"

Madeline's eyes widened. Had anyone else heard that question? Yes, a few teens straightened in their seats, and their gazes darted to her instead of their canvas.

"We're just friends," Madeline whispered back.

Flashing a bright, knowing grin, Florence didn't look like she believed her.

There was one way to stop further questions. So Madeline got up and walked along the aisles, looking at the paintings of different students. Florence didn't paint the still life with a vase and fruits on display. Instead, her work was a river on a sunny summer day with horses running on the riverbank. It was surprisingly cheerful, considering that, like Paisley, she'd never known her parents and had been left in a baby carrier at a Safe Haven.

According to Brandon, Florence's adoptive experience hadn't gone well. Her adoptive parents were okay. Then, later, a newly acquired adoptive sibling turned out to be abusive. Florence had run away, had been found and returned, and had run away again, labeled a troublemaker. Her adoptive parents didn't believe her. After she'd been beaten up and social services got involved again, she'd been removed from that family and passed from one set of foster parents to another ever since. Despite all that, she'd done well in school, unlike Tommy, who'd skipped school as much as he could.

Madeline's foster parents hadn't been great, but Madeline hadn't been passed from one home to another, which had allowed her to form a bond with her foster sisters. A bond that lasted through life and in many ways defined the best parts of her.

Neither Florence nor Tommy had that.

A band squeezed Madeline's rib cage, but she forced herself to move along. Most teens painted the still life. But about five of them depicted horses, and a few others worked on abstract pieces with cubes and triangles. She offered praise generously. Then she stopped at the last row and studied Tommy's painting.

Her eyes narrowed. Jagged lines slashed across the canvas in different hues of red to create a frightening overall effect, and she winced. What had this boy gone through? She only knew that his parents had lost parental rights when he'd been twelve, so it must've been bad.

He glared at her as if he didn't want her to look at his work, so she retreated to her seat, unsettled by his painting. Or was it something else? Maybe... maybe the scent? The combination of oil paints and... and eucalyptus, maybe? The latter might be from his shampoo. It reminded her of something, but what?

The memory didn't appear on demand. She had to accept that she still couldn't remember some things. Considering that the scent sent a shiver down her spine, perhaps because her brain was protecting her.

She did her best to shake off the feeling. Children and teens, like horses, could sense fear.

At least, she hadn't gotten any hostile comments or signs of mutiny, and she'd sort of expected them, considering the teens' history.

When she sat, Florence moved her easel closer still. Just great.

"Thank you for the gift. I've never had anything that nice," she whispered in Madeline's direction.

Madeline's heart softened. While she had humble beginnings, for several decades, she'd led a life of privilege. And yes, she'd survived betrayal, but she'd always known she could rely on her foster sisters.

Did this girl have anyone to rely on? This wasn't about the expensive purse. It was about showing that someone cared. The way Brandon had. The way the cowboy from the neighboring ranch, once a foster child and then a troubled teen himself, had organized this program in the first place.

Madeline might not know anything about teens or ranch life. But she knew well loss and despair and how the rug could be pulled from under her feet. And she knew shopping.

She remembered now how to choose a stylish dress, how to put on makeup. Well, except she hadn't used those skills today. Hmm. Brandon was right. A lot of kind things didn't even require much effort. Except for just being there for someone.

So after class, she asked Florence to stay. Brandon showed up five minutes before class was dismissed and was giving the students pointers now.

"If the project manager allows it, would you like to go shopping with me sometime?" Madeline asked Florence, then thought a moment. "We could get our nails done afterward."

Florence squealed loud enough for the entire building to hear her.

A pleasant feeling spread inside Madeline.

Brandon glanced in her direction and sent her a grateful smile, and that feeling intensified.

But she was still an outsider here, unlike Brandon, which was clear by the teens' open postures and animated talk with him. Except for Florence, they'd been silent with her, though they hadn't given her a hard time. To give them privacy, she edged from the classroom and waited for him in the hall.

Florence waved as she strode toward the exit, a new skip in her step. Tommy followed her at a distance, his shoulders hunched as if he tried to fold into himself. He probably still hadn't told Florence he liked her.

Then Madeline tensed as Tommy made a beeline for her.

Wait a moment. Waaaaait a moment.

She realized what bothered her so much about that scent of paint oil and eucalyptus. Because she knew now where she'd remembered that scent. That day was still blurry around the edges, but somehow the fragrance filtered through all the fog.

A new shiver tingled through her.

How hadn't she noticed at the parade when she'd first met Tommy? Oh, right. She didn't remember anything after coming to Cowboy Crossing then. And they'd been out in the open air, plus there had been an onslaught of many other scents.

She glanced at the ajar classroom door. Should she call for Brandon? Even better, run back to the class?

Or was she being paranoid?

Her hand slipped into her purse. The educational building was a weapons-free zone. But Arianna had insisted on Madeline taking at least a pocketknife. Madeline hadn't protested much. She was more comfortable with knives than guns. With a gunshot, she could miss. But as her memories and skills mostly came back, she knew precisely where to cut with a knife, depending on the purpose.

Hopefully, she was wrong about Tommy.

He stopped some distance away and looked up. With his hair falling into his eyes, reading him was difficult.

Her insides shook, but she straightened her spine just as her fingers tightened around the knife. Tommy didn't have the element of surprise on his side now. He couldn't be armed because all the students' backpacks were checked at the entrance, and as much as she disliked the metal detector, it served its purpose.

Besides, Brandon was only a few steps away, and Tommy and Madeline both knew it.

But then, she'd seen the damage even a shank could inflict, and it wasn't difficult to sharpen something into a shank. Could he be hiding one underneath his baggy T-shirt?

Okay. Okay.

Breathe.

Brandon was going to show up any minute. That gave her courage.

But why had Tommy attacked her? She was a stranger to him. Was it all about that diamond bracelet she'd been wearing? Had he wanted to give it to Florence, as well? But didn't he understand people would notice soon? It might even throw suspicion on Florence and make them think she'd stolen the bracelet.

Maybe Madeline was imagining things. Her memory was unreliable at best, and many pieces were still missing.

Thankful Tommy remained a safe distance away, she edged closer to the classroom door.

"You want to know why I struck you, don't you?" he asked.

Afraid her voice would betray her, she just nodded.

Brandon hurried to them, smiling, and her tight stomach muscles relaxed a tad. The rest of the students passed by, leaving the building.

The smile slipped off as Brandon must've felt the tension. "What's going on?"

Still hanging back, Tommy lifted his arms in a placating gesture. "I'm not gonna do anything." He sighed. "Mr. Brandon, I was the one who hit Ms. Madeline with a stone."

Brandon's jaw slackened. "How... how could you?" He positioned himself between them.

The teen sniffled. "I hated her." He spoke as if Madeline wasn't even there. "You're a good guy. You're one of the few ones who care for people like me. And she... she hurt you. We all saw how miserable you were after she broke up with you. It wasn't fair! People in town said she didn't care how many hearts she broke."

"That's not true," Madeline whispered, the words wrenching from her. "I didn't want to break anyone's heart. Much less Brandon's. He means too much to me."

Tommy didn't seem to listen. "Mom didn't care, either. Dad started drinking after she left. He gets really, really mean when he's drunk. Then he met someone, but she left, too. Dad got so much worse. I don't know what exactly happened.... I was at the park and saw Madeline. I became so, so angry. Like everything inside was going to explode. The next thing I knew, I had a rock in my hand."

Brandon placed his palms on the teen's shoulders. "I'm sorry about your parents. But that was no way to deal with the situation. If you talked to me or another adult here, we could've gotten you help."

The boy snorted. "Dad said real men don't ask for help."

"And how well did that work out for him?" Madeline asked softly. Or maybe she should've kept quiet. She'd never had great people skills. But then, apparently, she'd made others hate her without even talking to them.

"Not well at all." Tommy sniffled again. "You and Ms. Madeline are back together now. You look happy. I almost ruined it all for you."

Brandon squeezed Tommy's shoulders. "You know we'll have to go to the police now, right?"

"Yes."

Her gut twisted. The mystery of her assault was solved, but she didn't feel any satisfaction.

What Tommy had done was horrible, but he'd acted out of misguided loyalty to Brandon and misplaced anger at his parents. Matt Luettgen was still at large and just as set on revenge as Tommy had been. And she cringed at the reminder of having hurt Brandon so badly.

Even more, at the possibility of hurting him again.

Chapter Seventeen

MADELINE SANK INTO the living room couch three days later.

Jenna's face was impassive as she took a seat, but her striking blue eyes gave her away. Just a moment before she switched their expression to neutral, sadness filled them. Then she was all professional again. "I have some news I wanted to tell you in person."

Madeline's blood went cold. This had to be important. She moved the pink throw pillow separating her from Brandon and shifted closer to him along the couch as if needing support, then stopped herself. "Do you have the DNA test results?"

Just like the previous meeting with Jenna, Brandon was near Madeline, and his arm wrapped around her shoulder, giving her much-needed strength.

Jenna nodded. "That, too."

Oh, wow. So there was more.

An easy guess on the reason for the sadness in Jenna's eyes. "My dad... he wasn't my real father, was he?"

"I'm sorry. Do you want Salotto to know he is your father?" While Jenna's expression remained neutral, her voice softened. Her jet-black bangs fell on her eyes, and she swept them aside with an impatient gesture.

"I... I don't know yet," Madeline whispered. Her world tilted on its axis again.

She'd suspected the truth, and yet it was a shock to the system. She did have many qualities she'd thought she'd inherited from her father, from her dark hair to her talent for medicine to her tendency not to let anyone close. She didn't inherit them from him, after all.

She didn't even know the guy who'd fathered her. Considering she was a secret child, he might not want to get to know her.

Brandon's hand found hers. "I'll be there for you whatever you decide."

She gave him a grateful smile and didn't try to keep it from wobbling at the edges. "Eventually, I'd like to get to know Salotto better." She shuddered. "Unless, of course, he's the murderer."

Brandon squeezed her fingers but didn't say anything. He didn't need to.

"About that." Jenna's voice tightened.

Madeline froze. "Do you... do you already know?" Her pulse became erratic. Could the mystery of her entire life finally be solved? "Did you manage to solve a cold case that remained unsolved for decades?"

Jenna's lips curved slightly. "I can't take the credit, really. It was discovered by accident."

"By accident?" Madeline echoed, leaning closer to Brandon again. His embrace tightened, and Rusty moved to sit at her feet. She'd take "by accident." Could she now have the closure she'd been missing for so long?

"A colleague in Houston was hired to solve a crime, which he did, and the culprit was arrested. To get a more lenient sentence, the latter cut a deal and gave up his buddy who'd told him about murdering your parents. Nierling was arrested yesterday and confessed to the murder. He knew the crime-scene details and was a DNA match to a hair found in the lake house. It should be a solid case."

Madeline gasped as she tried to place the name and couldn't. "But why?" A whiny pleading laced her tone. "What was the motive? Robbery?"

Jenna hesitated. "That's the difficult part."

Her heart thudding, Madeline leaned forward. "Tell me. I'm not fragile. I have to know."

She was *not* the porcelain figurine about to shatter. Was she?

Brandon squeezed her fingers again, showing his support. She thought about asserting independence and moving away from him along the sofa. Instead, she laced her fingers through his. Something was to be said about facing life challenges together.

She'd thought she was too independent, thought no man was strong enough for her to lean on. But she was wrong. Brandon was such a man.

"Nierling claimed your father hired him."

Everything seemed to stop, freeze in time. Maybe she should've expected it. Yet her mind refused to believe it.

She could only gawk at Jenna, unwilling to comprehend the words. "This... this can't be true." Then Madeline's mind latched onto the logical thing. "It can't be. He got killed himself."

Jenna looked away. "Nierling claims it was his first murder. He was supposed to shoot your mom but only wound Mr. Wood. You know, to throw off any suspicion from him. After all, the spouse is always the primary suspect.

Nierling would take a few valuables and make it look like a robbery gone wrong. But he was so nervous his aim wasn't perfect. The slug hit a vital organ."

The words registered, but not fully. It was too horrific. The person she'd considered her father all her life had orchestrated the entire gruesome ordeal, not knowing it would go too far.

Even her happy memories of her childhood were an illusion. She had closure now, but it came at a high price.

It was too much to process, and her mind needed a distraction, even if a momentary one. "How are your children?"

Jenna's eyes widened as if she didn't expect this question.

Did Madeline overstep her boundaries? Her heart sank further. "I mean, if it's okay to ask."

Unlike for her foster sisters, social cues were difficult for Madeline to read. Of course, Jenna, who was professionalism exemplified, wouldn't welcome prying into her life, especially from a client she'd recently met. And Madeline must be wrong about the similarities between them.

Then Jenna's face, mostly dispassionate before, lit up, and her entire demeanor changed. "I never thought a toddler could create so much mess. Of course, she's still the best child in the world. And my son is such an awesome big brother. Did you know he wants to be an astronaut?" Obvious pride warmed her voice.

Madeline sighed out her relief. Jenna didn't mind a personal question. Of course, she didn't mention her difficult pregnancy or that she adopted her husband's nephew. One would think both were her biological children.

Madeline let out another slow breath. Maybe finding out who her biological father was wouldn't be so earth-shattering. At least, she'd have an alive one, even if he didn't want to know her, considering the circumstances. Maybe she should be grateful for the way the DNA test had turned out. She wouldn't want to be a killer's daughter.

It was all so frightening, so confusing.

Brandon squeezed her fingers again, and as her gaze roamed the now-familiar room with its built-in bookshelves and stone fireplace, she did her best to follow her foster sister's example and count her blessings. If she could accept his omission about their breakup—and she thought she could—he was so worthy of love.

But was she? As well as her being a mess, her family history was a mess. Was she a blessing to him or far from it?

She didn't know the answer, and that was an answer in itself.

He stayed with her after Jenna left, and they played in the yard with Rusty. But questions bounced in her mind like the ball she tossed—only Rusty wasn't there to retrieve them for her.

Once alone with Rusty, she took a deep breath and picked up her phone from the coffee table. Arianna was supposed to return any minute, and Madeline looked forward to talking to her. But once the danger passed and Matt Luettgen was apprehended, Arianna would leave. Not because she didn't care, but because something in her needed constant movement.

Madeline welcomed memories of times with their other foster sisters who were appearing more and more now. For so long, the only friendships she had were with her foster sisters. Maybe because she'd given off that arrogant vibe and people stayed away from her. With her already being considered unapproachable, the nature of her job didn't help matters. She'd been respected in a professional sense, and she'd persuaded herself it was enough. The few people who'd tried to get close to her she'd pushed away. She'd never reached out for friendship herself.

But despite all Jenna's professionalism, Madeline had sensed a kindred spirit. She wanted to see the photos of Jenna's children, with the girl sure to become a little fashionista. They shared their affection for art and fashion. Jenna seemed foreign to the ranch world, despite growing up here, but after decades in Europe, she'd readjusted to life on the ranch—something Madeline wanted to learn.

Her gut twisted. Could she ask for friendship now? Could she put herself out that way?

She pulled her shoulders back. Only one way to find out.

But Jenna had a busy life. And Madeline was still her client. And Jenna knew what a mess Madeline was, how much baggage she carried. And... Madeline pressed dial before she could talk herself out of it.

Once Jenna answered, Madeline started talking fast. "I hope I'm not calling too late. And you might be busy. And I know I'm still your client, but once that's over... Would you like to meet up for coffee? Or go to some art exhibition in Springfield?"

Or should she have suggested shopping? Or nothing at all?

Madeline cringed. "It's probably not a good idea. I shouldn't have asked."

"I'd love to," Jenna said.

As Brandon and Madeline walked together in the fields, daisies dancing at their feet, he took her hand. She stilled but didn't remove hers, and he was grateful. His heartbeat picked up a notch at their proximity. He realized now that physical contact—well, emotional contact, too—was difficult for her. Her letting him close was a privilege he didn't take for granted.

But could he fully commit to her if she wasn't a Christian? And how could she commit to him if she wasn't going to stay in Cowboy Crossing?

His heart wrenched.

Forgive me, Lord. It's selfish to want her to become a believer so we could have a chance to be together.

But with her receiving horrible news about her family mystery, with Matt Luettgen still out there bent on revenge, Brandon couldn't walk away yet, either.

He didn't want to walk away at all.

Despite all his best intentions, she'd become his world. He already couldn't imagine his life without her.

"I pray you find happiness." He squeezed her hand. "I pray for your healing. I know that discovery about your father was heartbreaking."

"Thank you." She dipped her head, her luscious hair slipping forward before she shook it back over her shoulders. "I thought a lot about what you told me about God. I read books. I watched movies. I talked to Jessie and Paisley, who became believers. I searched my heart."

"What did you decide?" He prayed to God for the answer Brandon so desperately needed to hear. Then he held his breath.

"I still can't understand many things. Like the reason for human suffering. But at the same time, I know how much I need God's love. Maybe it's the wrong reason to seek God. Would that disappoint Him? What if He decides I'm too beyond repair to be loved?"

So much turmoil roiled those eyes the color of the sky above them. He barely resisted the urge to take her in his arms.

"God loves you as you are. You're not a disappointment to Him. All you need to do is to accept His love."

Her face lit up, her eyes becoming luminous. "Okay, I still have to think about it. But I am leaning toward becoming a Christian."

Elated, he hugged her, but then made an effort to let her go.

His lungs filled with the grassy, sun-warmed earth scent of joy, his chest expanding until he feared one couldn't contain such emotion. He'd never felt as at peace as he did at this moment. And he realized a simple truth as if it were written in the sky.

He loved her.

Could he tell her that, though?

He couldn't let it affect her decision to leave. He wouldn't want her to sacrifice her happiness for his. She longed for fulfillment and purpose, and he couldn't affect her journey.

Lord, please guide her.

Her gaze traveled to the horses in the distance. Then she bent down, plucked one of the tall daisies, and tucked it behind one ear. "I know what I'm going to name the little foal. And the newborn one, if that's okay."

He grinned. "Of course, it's okay." Thankfully, the new foal's mother hadn't rejected her, so she didn't have to be bottle-fed.

Madeline stuck out her hand as if she were trying to hold onto the wind, and frankly, that was the way he felt with her sometimes.

"It's a weird feeling, but it's like this land started speaking to me," she said. "Like I can find my place here. I loved working with the horses. I can't wait to see calves when they are born. I can't teach art to troubled teens, but maybe I can teach them, I don't know, first aid. Provide a sympathetic ear. I want to volunteer at the center."

"I'd love that. But you have a medical diploma and had a spectacular career in Houston." A bird flew out from the grass as if spooked by their footfalls, and he watched it in the sky.

Hurt dimmed Madeline's eyes. "The man I considered my father had both, but it didn't make him happy." She kept silent as if processing that was still difficult for her.

Nodding, he forced himself to voice the obvious. "But there was more than your job to your previous life. We don't have fancy parties here. Or opera and theater."

"Oh, please." She rolled her eyes. "While I like opera and the theater, they're not necessities for me. And I never liked fancy parties—or any parties, for that matter. I feel uncomfortable among too many people. Or around people, period."

As she shivered, the daisy fell from behind her ear.

He stooped and caught it, handing it back, wishing he could give her everything she needed or would ever want.

"What is a necessity for you?" His heart thumped. Was his life about to change today? Could she call this place home? Could she open herself to his love?

He wanted to spend a lifetime with her. Helping her heal. Loving her. Cherishing her.

She plucked a petal from the flower. "Well, my foster sisters are very important to me." Another petal fell away. "Jessie is already here. Paisley is going to move to your family ranch in a year when her husband leaves the army. Arianna is staying at the lodge for now, though probably not for long."

Petals drifted from her fingers with each sentence. *She loves me; she loves me not....* The singsong words pulsed through his head with each discarded petal.

"And you..." she murmured. Only one petal remained. She plucked it too, holding onto this one while the stem tumbled to the ground. "You're here."

He looked into her eyes, afraid to believe it. *She loves me....* "Am I important to you?"

"You have no idea." Her eyes became vulnerable, and this time, she didn't try to hide it.

Could he tell her that he loved her? That he wanted to marry her? Have children with her?

He'd hidden their breakup from her, and look how that had turned out. He had to be honest, even if it made him vulnerable in return.

He dropped on one knee into the daisies and tall meadow grasses. He didn't have a ring yet, but he had the words he needed to say. "I love you. Everything I know about you and everything I'm about to discover. You aren't too broken to love. Far from it. I love every jagged piece of your soul."

Her eyes went huge. "Or could it be you just loved helping me?"

"I did, but there's so much more to it than that. I love you for your strength, not your weakness. I've seen none of the latter. You survived so much and still have such a beautiful soul." He anticipated her next question. "Because you're not just gorgeous on the outside, though there's that. You have such a beautiful soul that I'm still in awe I have the chance to get to know you."

Her lips trembled. "How can you be so sure?"

"Because I am. If you return my feelings... If you think you can be happy here... Will you marry me?"

Tears streamed down her face. "I don't want to hurt you again. I... I can't." Then she turned around, flicked the last petal from her fingers, and ran away.

She loves me not. The child's singsong game mocked him as he let her go, his heart shattering for the second time.

Well, it was better to do something constructive than sulk and cry after rejecting Brandon's proposal. Madeline could bake. Her foster sisters might enjoy a pie. Which meant she needed to buy ingredients.

She had a quick breakfast with Arianna, Genevieve, and Gold. The latter two had then left for Springfield.

Madeline didn't mention grocery shopping. Arianna would need convincing again that Madeline wasn't a little girl who needed a chaperone while going to buy apples and flour. She looked up a recipe online, put the gun from the safe into her purse, then drove to the grocery store, grateful for the tinted windows in her flashy car. After her karaoke fiasco, she didn't want people in town to see her.

She bought things quickly, reluctant to be stopped and asked about it. Then she placed groceries in the trunk and hurriedly slid into the driver's seat. But when she took out her keys, her hand froze in the air.

Wait a moment.

What was that strange scent? Liquor? She didn't drink, so how...

The cold metal of a gun stuck in the back of her neck made her shudder.

A raspy whisper traveled to her ear. "Don't scream if you don't want to get shot."

Chapter Eighteen

EVERYTHING INSIDE MADELINE went cold. She gasped for air like a fish thrown onto the ice.

"What do you want?" She didn't recognize her voice. It came out as a squeak, so she asked again, firmer this time. "My diamond bracelet?"

She had a gun in her purse, but it wasn't like she could aim at him in the back seat. Never mind that, by the time she drew her gun, her brains could be on the car ceiling. She shuddered again, now rethinking her gratitude about tinted windows. To avoid people, she'd also parked in the farthest corner of the parking lot. *Just great.*

Maybe wearing expensive jewelry wasn't such a great idea. If she got out of this alive...

She didn't finish that thought because the gun jabbed her harder as the guy let out a dark chuckle. "This is not about jewelry. Though, on the other hand, it wouldn't hurt. Hand over your bracelet, then start driving to your house."

Not a good sign. She'd prefer a simple theft.

The voice sounded vaguely familiar. Oh yes.

Matt Luettgen. He'd caught up with her. She'd even failed at protecting herself.

Such thinking wasn't going to help.

There should be a way out of this. She still had so much life to live. Now all the obstacles that had kept her away from Brandon didn't seem so important.

She should've said yes to his proposal. She loved him. Not the best time to realize it, but now when all her defenses were stripped bare, the fog of doubt cleared, and she had sudden clarity.

She might have minutes to live, and the biggest regret in her life was that she'd pushed away the man she loved instead of telling him how she felt.

She was terrified now. But she'd been afraid when Brandon had proposed to her, too. Afraid that eventually he'd be disappointed in her like her father—the man she'd thought was her father—had been, just as her ex had been. That once she'd accepted Brandon's love and proposal, losing him would hurt too much. That she wouldn't be able to survive that.

"Drive faster!" Luettgen growled behind her.

She pressed the gas pedal, but not much. She should be thinking of a way out, of a way to reach for her gun in the purse on the front passenger seat. Instead, her mind drifted to Brandon.

She should've taken that risk with him. He knew she wasn't just a pretty face. He didn't hold illusions about her but accepted her the way she was. She was real with him. Maybe he wouldn't be disappointed in her.

And she wasn't just a project to him. Once she'd regained most of her memory, he hadn't moved on to someone else or something else. Instead, he'd wanted to spend a lifetime with her.

Yet she'd said no. A knife sliced into her chest.

She drove up to the gate. She still had no clue what to do. The cameras inside and outside the lodge wouldn't help her if she were dead.

She punched in the code, and the gate opened. Could she make a run for it once she neared the house? Not with the gun poking into her. She shuddered again.

Then she realized such a simple truth that it struck her how she hadn't seen it before. She'd asked Brandon why he loved her as if she needed to earn his love first. Like she'd tried to do with the man she'd considered her father and later with her ex. She'd pushed people away because she'd thought she didn't deserve their love and they would be disappointed once they figured it out.

But she didn't need to earn love or deserve it. Just like Brandon didn't need to earn or deserve her love.

She could be loved and cherished as she was.

Brandon had said that God loved her. That she didn't need to earn that love. It was there already. She just needed to accept it.

Lord, if You hear me now... I accept Your love. Please, please help me survive this, and I'll accept Brandon's love. That is, if he'll still have me.

Just great. She'd only sought God in a time of need. Shouldn't she have done it sooner? She was such a disappointment.

Stop.

God loved her.

Even if she wasn't perfect. Even if sometimes she didn't love herself much.

She stopped shivering. Her blood was still cold, and terror grasped her windpipe and squeezed. But, at the same time, she could breathe now.

"Park close to the house," Luettgen ordered.

"Okay." Her voice wasn't trembling any longer, either.

She needed to keep him talking. Engaged. If Arianna checked the cameras on her phone, she'd know what was going on and call the police.

Madeline turned off the engine and moved her hand to her purse. She still had a chance to get her gun. "You know that, even if I didn't testify, you'd still have been sentenced to go to jail."

"Shut up! You ruined my life! Go to the house and open the front door. Don't even think about running." He snatched her purse from the front seat.

So much for trying to get the weapon. She clenched her teeth. She could dart into the house while he opened the car, but she'd be an easy target. "I was just doing my job."

"Move! I'm running out of patience. You don't want me to go after Genevieve and her daughter, too, do you?"

No, she didn't. The threat made her move toward the front door and unlock it. He'd be caught eventually. And once he was inside, Rusty would pounce on him. A loud bark greeted them. Rusty was ready.

"Disable the alarm," Luettgen growled. "Make sure you tell your dog to stay still. Or I'll shoot him."

Cold traveled down her spine. No, no, no. She couldn't do that to Rusty. She stepped inside and, in the sternest voice possible, told him to sit.

Rusty growled, and his hackles rose. But he sat. He looked ready to jump the moment she gave the command.

Her heart pounded in her chest. She disabled the alarm. There was still hope. She had to stay alive. She could use something heavy in the living room to hit him with and run along with Rusty. The doors in many of the rooms locked from the inside and were bulletproof. They even had a safe room downstairs. She still had her phone from which she could call for help.

Brandon and his brothers would be here in a heartbeat. They'd figure out what to do. Besides, once she escaped, Luettgen might simply leave.

"Move forward." His gun jammed into her side painfully, sure to leave bruises.

She'd be grateful if bruises were all she got out of this. She walked into the living room, surveying the place for anything heavy. Or sharp. "It's still not too late. No harm was done. You can still leave. Go on with your life."

"No, it's too late. You've got to pay for what you've done." His voice dropped as if resigned.

Rusty followed them, his ear pricked up on high alert, and she told him to stay again. Then she sent up a prayer for her dog.

"Turn around. I want to see your face. I want to see you scared."

Well, he was going to be unpleasantly surprised. Chin high, she turned around and glared at him. Due to her height, they were almost on the same level.

His mouth twisted.

Good.

This change also meant the gun wasn't pressed to her ribs any longer. Though it was still trained on her, she called it an improvement.

"It's the other way around," she said with all the calmness she could muster. "You're the one scared."

"Shut up!"

A letter opener rested underneath a few envelopes on the coffee table. If she couldn't find anything else, could that work? She knew well where all the important arteries were. And she was great with sharp objects. She could do a lot of damage fast if she had to.

In this case, she had to.

"I only did my job!" she said again, inching closer to the coffee table. Still too far, but she could dart for it.

Then she heard voices outside. Genevieve and her daughter.

Madeline's stomach dropped into the carpet. If it were Arianna, she'd be armed and alert, but Genevieve and Gold might not be.

"Madeline, we're home!" Genevieve's cheerful voice made Madeline flinch.

Luettgen sighed. "I guess I'll have to shoot more people today than I intended to."

She couldn't let that happen. The letter opener was still too far away. Footfalls in the hall reached her. In the next second, they'd be here.

She stepped in front of the gun the moment Rusty launched.

Brandon spent the day nursing his wounds among the horses. Then he drove to Springfield to pick up tack.

But even though she'd rejected it, he didn't regret his proposal. He regretted his haste. Madeline wasn't ready.

Unlike the first time, he wasn't going to give up on her. She'd said she had growing feelings for him, so he'd wait for her for however long it took for them, well, to grow enough.

While she was alive, there was hope.

He'd barely left the city when his phone rang. Ronan. Brandon answered on his hands-free phone. "Hello, Ronan."

After a pause, his brother appeared on the line. "I shouldn't be telling you this, but... We got a call from Genevieve at the lodge. There was a shootout."

"What?" Brandon swerved but managed to straighten out the truck. He couldn't have heard that right. How could anyone enter that fortress? "Is Madeline okay?" He should ask about the others, of course. "Are her foster sisters okay? And Rusty?"

"Genevieve is fine, and Arianna wasn't home at the time. The German shepherd is fine, too. Madeline was shot at. Close range. I have to go now. I'll call back when I know more." Ronan disconnected.

For a few seconds, Brandon went numb and somehow managed to stay on the road. He should pull up to the side and regroup, but he needed to be at the lodge as soon as possible.

His insides went cold, and he prayed more than he'd ever prayed in his life. Mostly, it was repeating the same word now.

Please, please, please.

If something happened to her...

He'd even accept it if he had to live his life without her if only she were alive. Even if she were happy with someone else. He loved her that much.

He pressed on the gas pedal and weaved in and out of traffic. He was usually a law-abiding citizen and didn't go above the speed limit, but he needed to get to Madeline. To make sure she was okay.

His fingers tightened around the steering wheel so hard his knuckles whitened.

Please, please, please.

The way from Springfield to Cowboy Crossing seemed to last an eternity, and every second beat painfully in his temple.

A few miles from the lodge, he checked his phone and frowned. It was turned off. The battery must've run out of juice. Of all times!

That meant, if Ronan or anyone from his family had tried to call, they wouldn't be able to reach him. He punched the code and entered the gate.

There were no patrol cars with flashing lights or ambulances, though there were plenty of other vehicles, and he didn't know whether that was a good sign or not. His heart about stopped as he leaped out of the truck. Then it started pounding with excruciating force. He didn't even shut the truck door but bolted to the house and took all the front porch steps in one giant leap.

Arianna opened the door. She probably saw him on the camera. Barking sounded behind her.

He didn't waste time on greetings. "How's Madeline? Can I see her?"

Arianna shook her head. "She's gone—"

Chapter Nineteen

NO, NO, NO.

That couldn't be true. He staggered.

Arianna stepped out onto the porch. "Are you okay?"

He snatched the railing to keep standing. "How can I be okay when you just said…"

"Well, you can't see her because she's gone to see you."

"She what?" Relief overwhelmed him, but his emotions had swung so much today that he needed to make sure.

Arianna tilted her head. "Maybe we let the paramedics go too soon."

"Please tell me she's okay. I heard there was a shootout here."

"Yes. Come on in. On the other hand, there are tons of people here, so it's better to talk in the yard."

He didn't care where they talked, so he followed her to the yard. Okay, maybe he did care. He was more comfortable outdoors.

"I'll make this short," Arianna said. "Matt Luettgen kidnapped Madeline in the grocery store parking lot and forced entry into the lodge while holding her at gunpoint. When Genevieve and Gold entered the lodge, from what I understand, Madeline stepped forward to take a bullet for them. But Rusty lunged at Luettgen, and the guy misfired."

That sounded like a miracle. "Thank You, Lord! So no one was hurt?"

Arianna shrugged. "Just Matt Luettgen. He has a nasty bite wound. The ambulance was for him." She didn't sound sorry at all. "Your brother arrested him and took Madeline's and Genevieve's statements."

"So she's fine," Brandon repeated as if it made it more… more true maybe.

Arianna looked at him as if he indeed needed medical help. "Yes." Then she rolled her eyes. "Sadly, I missed everything."

Did she wish she'd been the one confronting the gunman? Weird.

He must be reading into things. Then joy inflated his lungs. "That means the threat is gone." It also meant Madeline wouldn't need him and his protection as much any longer. Not that he'd done a great job at protecting her.

While a speck of sadness touched him at that, Madeline had a point. He didn't need to help people to be liked and compensate for his grouchy character. He could be loved for who he was. If only Madeline could love him like that.

Arianna seemed to read his previous thoughts. "She still needs you. Even if she doesn't realize it now, she will one day."

He prayed she was right. "I'm not going anywhere. Except to find Madeline."

Arianna's mouth tipped up a tad. "Good. Okay, I'd better get inside. Lots of people showed up, including from your family. With casseroles! And tons of treats for Rusty. Somehow, they think we need comforting after a little shootout." She shook her head as if not understanding that concept, then strode to the porch.

He hurried to his truck.

Arianna was a remarkable woman, and he understood his brother's attraction to her now. But like Brandon, Kieran was a cowboy who loved their ranch and a family man dreaming of a stable life with a wife and children. Unable to imagine Arianna settling down with a husband and children, Brandon said a quick prayer for his brother.

Then his thoughts switched to Madeline. He pulled out of the parking space and soon was on the road.

Where would she go to look for him? And why would she do that in the first place? His heartbeat kicked up. Could he hope she'd changed her mind? Or was that wishful thinking?

His house would be the first logical place to look, so he stopped there. But he didn't find her flashy red car nearby, and his stomach tightened.

Next was the stable, and one of the cowhands told him he'd just missed her.

He rushed to his parents' home. His mother met him with a pie in her hands. "Madeline was just here ten minutes ago, looking for you." Based on the joy in her voice, she was reading too much into it. "Let's go to that poor family. They could use some comfort food. And maybe she went back there."

He knew where his affinity to help people came from. He took the pie from her as its wonderful aroma spread around them. "Thank you."

Then Mom studied him. "Hold on. What happened between you two? I was going to ask you earlier, but you drove off to Springfield too fast."

Their mother always read them like open books. "Yesterday, I told her I loved her and proposed, and she said no." He frowned.

"Well, if she was running around today looking for you after nearly being shot, that might be a good sign. Not her being shot, but her looking for you. Wait here." She disappeared into the hall and returned with a box. "Here. It's not my engagement ring, but it's a family heirloom. It's not fancy, but—"

"Thank you." He accepted the box and slipped it into his pocket while balancing the covered pie in one hand. He'd thought Madeline liked fancy things, but he was wrong. Maybe in a few years she'd say yes to marriage with this ring. Hopefully sooner than a decade.

With the distance to the lodge so short, they made it there in a flash.

Please let her be here.

Arianna opened the front door again and waved them in. She must be watching those cameras extra carefully now.

His heart stuttered as he saw Madeline in the crowd of townspeople, her posture stiff. As if feeling his gaze, she turned around. She froze for a moment.

Then she rushed to him. Somehow, Arianna managed to intercept the covered dish seconds before Madeline flung her arms around him.

"Thank you for the pie. I'll go put it on the table. Please join us for some treats—I don't mean dog treats—when you're done hugging." Arianna walked away.

Emotions swirled inside him. Wonder, wistfulness, surprise, and so much more. It was unusual for Madeline as she'd never clung to him in public. Or alone, for that matter. His heart swelled. Then he wrapped his arms around her, cherishing the moment.

"I'm so glad you're okay," he whispered in her hair.

He wanted to say how much he loved her, but he'd already told her and made her flee.

Then she freed herself from his embrace and glanced back at the crowd. She probably regretted her display of affection. Did what people thought still matter to her so much?

She took a deep breath and dropped to one knee.

He stared at her. "What are you doing?"

All conversations around them quieted, and people moved closer.

"I love you, Brandon O'Neill. I don't know why it took so much time and a gun to my head to realize it. I love how much you care for me and others, your passion for art, your love for family. But first and foremost, I love you."

Overwhelming joy swallowed him whole, but he tried to help her up. He knew how much it cost her to put herself out there like that, especially in public. "I love you very much, too."

Her smile was luminous. "Still?"

"Forever." He tried to lift her to her feet.

She shook her head. "I'm not done here yet. I want to spend a lifetime with you. Will you marry me please?"

Everyone gasped, including him. Could he believe his deepest desire was about to come true? But hadn't she said no to his proposal just yesterday?

He sank onto his knees near her. "Are you sure?"

Kieran cleared his throat. "That's not a very good answer, bro."

Arianna sighed. "It wasn't even an answer, but a question."

"I'm sure. I'm absolutely sure. Make me the happiest woman alive. Marry me." Madeline looked into his eyes, hers misty. With so much love shining there, he couldn't speak.

Then worry and embarrassment filled her eyes, and Kieran cleared his throat again.

"Yes. Yes! Yes. I want to marry you so badly." His hands shook as he reached into his pocket and fished out the box, grateful for his mother's foresight.

But what if they were wrong and Madeline didn't like it? He'd seen some of her jewelry. It was spectacular.

He opened the box. "This is an heirloom ring my mother gave me for you."

Tears filled her eyes. She moved her hand toward him, and he slipped the ring on her finger. Then she tucked it close to her heart. "It means so much to me."

His whole being elated, he got up and helped her stand while people applauded. Two miracles happened today, and he was immensely grateful to God for them both.

Three weeks later...

Madeline promised herself she wasn't going to compare her first wedding with her current one. Yet she did.

When she'd gotten married the first time, she'd wanted it to be perfect. After all, her fiancé was an important person about to run for public office. He had a lot of influential people to impress. After a painful divorce, she'd wondered whether she'd just been that to him, something beautiful to impress people.

The reception then had been at an elegant but outrageously expensive venue with chandeliers and columns and entrées she couldn't even pronounce. Champagne had been flowing like a river, a river weaving around guests in tuxedos or evening gowns while diamonds had sparkled on its surface.

A famous designer had designed her dress with a fit so tight she'd felt it suffocating her. Between the final fitting and the wedding, she'd been afraid even to breathe the scent of bread and gain weight.

Her fiancé insisted on her taking dance lessons for two months because, apparently, she'd had two left feet, and they'd needed to look great for their first dance. Smoke filled the dance floor then as a celebrity singer crooned, and the same smoke mixed with dizziness had filled her brain. A professional makeup artist and a world-famous hairdresser from her model days had corroborated on her hair and makeup. But the elegant updo had made her scalp itch while the astronomical insurance on her diamond necklace nearly choked her, and she'd shuddered at the thought of losing it somehow.

Her designer stilettoes had given her blisters, but she'd kept up her smile until, hours later, she'd collapsed at their new home and practically poured blood out of her sparkly shoes.

She'd been a bundle of nerves at the ceremony and then at the reception, unable to eat or drink. But she'd attributed it to a bride's nervous jitters. Now she knew that her heart—and fine, also her stomach—had been telling her she'd made a huge mistake.

Today, she waited for jitters as Florence spread white rose petals along the aisle. Florence had surprised Madeline by volunteering to be a flower girl, though her age had surpassed the regular age for it several times over. But Florence had never been a flower girl, and Madeline had been happy to accept.

Madeline smiled. She'd done a lot of thinking these last few weeks, researching, and talking with Brandon. Once she'd started volunteering at the troubled teens' center, including giving cooking lessons or simply a friendly ear, she'd gotten attached to Florence and the other girls. After tutoring Florence in chemistry and biology, Madeline was amazed by how bright the girl was and suggested Florence become a doctor. Madeline would do everything to help her on that path. But once Florence began working with calves and foals, the girl set her heart on becoming a veterinarian, which made Liberty proud. Liberty was volunteering now at the program, too.

Brandon and Madeline decided to apply to the foster program to become foster parents, and it felt right. They'd even thought about adopting Florence, but that was something they were still discussing. Growing up in the foster system, Madeline had known how heartbreaking it was to know nobody wanted her, nobody cared. She'd always thought one of the girls from their makeshift family would become a foster parent someday but didn't think it would be her.

She hadn't thought she'd had enough warmth in her heart, but loving Brandon had made her realize she had plenty. Of course, she knew the difficulties she was about to encounter, and Tommy's example was a stark reminder of that.

Her heart squeezed painfully. Florence, many other foster teens, and Madeline and Brandon testified on Tommy's behalf and were awaiting the outcome. While she believed his actions had to have consequences, she'd forgiven the teen and wanted him to turn his life around, hopefully without hitting her on the head again. Brandon raised funds to hire more counselors for the center, and Tommy was going through therapy. He'd been remorseful, and she hoped it wasn't too late for him. She prayed he'd get community service as his eventual sentence. She didn't know whether she'd be ready to become a foster mom for him yet though, so she prayed for guidance on that.

She'd started therapy, too. Her foster parents had never bothered to take her to a therapist, and treating the childhood trauma that had kept its hold on her throughout her life was long overdue. She could've asked for help when she'd grown up, but she'd been too afraid to appear damaged. Imperfect. Vulnerable.

Once she'd understood how precious her memories were, she'd allowed herself to analyze them instead of trying to push them away and was able to get better. She knew now not to blame herself for the death of the person she'd considered her father.

She also finally remembered the words he'd whispered before dying, and it wasn't the name of the culprit like she'd thought.

Forgive me.

With the therapist's help and Brandon's gentle assistance, she did, indeed, forgive him—and herself.

Jenna walked down the aisle in a dress she'd made herself that was as stylish as the woman herself. She'd helped with the decorations and agreed to be Madeline's bridesmaid. Despite their busy schedules, they'd become fast friends and now regularly met up for coffee or a trip to an art gallery.

Then Ronan and Jessie walked ahead of Madeline down the makeshift aisle in Brandon's parents' backyard, the fragrance of wildflowers greeting her. She waited for cloudiness and dizziness and a painfully clenched stomach like at her first wedding. But all she felt was overwhelming joy, no confusion or pain. No uncertainty. She couldn't wait to marry Brandon, who waited for her in a button-down shirt, a white cowboy hat, gray slacks, and cowboy boots. She loved him with her whole heart and had no doubt he loved her in the same way.

She didn't know yet what her future would hold, but she'd found her purpose and fulfillment in a small town in the Show Me state and in Brandon's heart.

This wedding was the opposite of her first one in so many senses. There were no evening gowns in sight now, and people dressed in their Sunday best. No half-a-year preparation. One couldn't compare the modest backyard with the ornate banquet hall. But it was filled with wildflowers and genuine smiles, and that mattered more to her. The guests brought mismatched chairs from their own houses, somehow opening their hearts and hearths and homes to her in the process, and that, in turn, opened her heart to them, as well.

Her dress flowed on her body instead of constricting her. Brandon's mom had offered her wedding dress, and Madeline gratefully accepted, even if it was a bit yellowed from age. She'd surprised herself by deciding to go barefoot, and soft grass caressed her feet as Arianna and Genevieve flanked her and they moved forward.

Brandon's father had offered to give her away, causing thankful tears in her eyes, but when she was little, she'd decided Genevieve would give her away at her wedding. She hadn't had that chance at her first wedding because her ex had thought it inappropriate. Instead, she'd walked the aisle alone, holding back tears that had been anything but thankful.

The breeze caressed the hair she'd let flow over her shoulders. Instead of diamonds, Jessie had helped her decorate it with wildflowers like Paisley had done as a bride.

Brandon's parents smiled at her from their seats, and his mom swiped a tear. They'd told her Brandon had changed for the better in the last three weeks, no longer the grouch he could be sometimes. She didn't think it was her influence, but she was glad he was taking more time for himself and his art. She loved him for his generosity, but she didn't want him to burn out. Where she'd needed to become a little less selfish, he'd needed to become a little less selfless and let others help carry his burdens. And she loved sharing his cares, his joys, and yes, his burdens as much as he seemed to love sharing hers.

She didn't know all the people in those endearing chairs. Brandon and his family were obviously well-loved here. Then her step faltered as she recognized the tall man with salt-and-pepper hair from the photo Jenna had emailed her. Salotto. Madeline's biological father.

Their eyes met, and a touch of warmth glowed in those eyes the same shade as her own. Or maybe she imagined it.

When she'd called him with the news about her parentage, he hadn't believed her. Or hadn't wanted to. Her insides still churned when she'd thought about her origin, though it was no fault of hers, so she imagined he felt even more shame. But if she needed other people to accept her the way she was, she had to cut others some slack, too. Her heart squeezed. Calling him to invite him to the wedding might've been a mistake. She didn't want to complicate his life, but he was the only blood relative she had left.

Then he looked away.

Okay then. She continued her walk, holding her head high. Though she wanted to get to know him better and through him to have more memories of her mother, she'd be fine if he rejected her. It didn't make her a failure as she'd once thought her father's rejection had. She was *not* a disappointment. On the opposite, she'd been learning to love herself the way Brandon loved her.

Maybe even the way God loved her.

She'd been devastated over losing her biological family for so long that she hadn't fully appreciated the family of the heart that was right in front of her.

She knew better now. Losing her memories and learning her life anew before they returned had made her see how blessed she was to have her foster sisters. And Brandon and his caring family had accepted her into their fold with no questions asked. They'd been there for her even when she'd been cold and distant, and in doing so, they'd broken down the high fence she'd constructed around her heart.

They all loved her unconditionally, and that let her love flow. They were her family now. Her dream. Her life.

The sun shone warm upon her, but she wouldn't be bothered if it rained. It would extinguish the flames if someone set her hair on fire again like Paisley had at her wedding. Paisley and her husband had flown in from Germany, and Madeline's circle of best friends and sisters of the heart was complete.

Her fingers moved to the cross on her neck, which together with a silver chain and the heirloom ring were the only jewelry she wore today.

Her chest swelled, though she didn't think any more joy could fill it as Brandon met her at the end of the aisle. Admiration shone in his eyes, but respect and acceptance gleamed there, as well. He knew her faults and embraced them instead of concentrating on her outer beauty. He hadn't let her push him away even when she'd hurt him, and that still floored her.

His smile brightened her world, and it always would.

Epilogue

"I HAVE A HALF SISTER?" Arianna stared at the police officer. She wasn't surprised often in life, but this news nearly rendered her speechless.

"Had. She was your father's child. She died after an accident. I'm very sorry for your loss. But you do have a nephew and a niece."

Now there wasn't anything *nearly* about it. Arianna *was* speechless. Her mouth slackened until she must resemble a fish thrown out of the water, gasping for air. She did her best to comprehend it.

Granted, she'd cut all ties to her family after parental rights had been taken from her parents and she'd been placed in the foster system. The half sister must've been born after that.

Someone she'd never known and now never would. The sense of loss was strong, considering the woman was a stranger, someone Arianna would've passed on the street without recognizing. And those poor children...

Her gaze moved to the short-haired woman in a strict navy suit who'd introduced herself as a social worker, and Arianna's mind whirled. The reason for her presence here...

No, hopefully not.

"Is the children's father going to take care of them?" Arianna licked her dry lips.

"The children's father or fathers are unknown," the social worker said, her voice weary.

What about Arianna's father?

Right. She shuddered and placed the memory deep where it belonged, in a far corner of her mind that should have three locks and an alarm system to get to it. Even if her father was still living, he wouldn't qualify to take care of children. She wouldn't trust him with a rat. Though a rat might've recognized a kindred spirit in her dad.

Then it registered. *Hold on.* Was she expected to take in the children?

"Will you consider adopting the children?" the social worker asked.

Arianna shook her head so violently long hair slapped her cheeks. There had been a reason she'd avoided romantic entanglements all these years.

Avoided getting attached, except to her foster sisters, and even there she'd set boundaries. Kept secrets.

Including one that was going to haunt her forever. Pain sliced through her.

Something had broken inside her. Something very necessary to form a family. To survive, she'd numbed her feelings. To become what she was now. There was no way back from that.

She shook her head again. "I can't. I can't! I... I travel a lot. I don't have a permanent home." It didn't make sense to have one with all her travels. She'd just received a new assignment for a remote location in Asia. A risky one, but that was her favorite thing about the assignment. Happily married now, Madeline didn't need her help any longer with the mystery behind her assault solved and another threat eliminated. After her wonderful wedding, Madeline had moved into Brandon's ranch house. It was a pity to leave the large lodge empty, but some things couldn't be helped. Arianna had stayed in one place long enough and had the unmistakable itch to move again.

She'd learned early that it was much more difficult to catch a person who was moving fast.

Guilt stabbed her. The children... No. It would be better if someone else stepped in. Children needed someone warm and cuddly. Someone with a safe profession and no emotional and physical scars. She was anything but.

"Isn't there anyone else who can take care of them?" Unfamiliar-to-her desperation sounded in her voice. She cringed. She'd promised herself she'd never be desperate again.

The social worker frowned. "There's one more option. Your cousin. He's married now, so it might be a better option."

Everything inside Arianna shuddered, and her heart did a one-eighty. He'd never gotten punished because she hadn't any proof.

Her world upside down now, she leveled her gaze on her visitors, then shocked herself by saying, "No. No! He can't have them. That's not going to happen."

"It's better than letting them go into the foster system."

Right. Right! And she'd just refused to take the children in. Because she wasn't fit to be a mother, among other reasons. And one of her previous assignments hadn't ended well. If she was tracked down, could it put her in danger? Much worse, could it put the children in danger? She was sure she'd covered her tracks well, but life had no guarantees.

She was as far from a good mother figure as Asia was from the Show Me state.

But the alternative... She suppressed another shudder. She couldn't let that happen. She raised her chin and heard herself saying, "I'll take care of the children. What do I need to do to win custody?"

The sudden decision affected her like a bucket of cold water. But she couldn't change it. She wouldn't let innocent children go through what happened to her. Pain knifed her, dragging her into the abyss of memories, but she held onto the edge of the cliff. She'd survived before, but barely.

The social worker blinked while the police officer studied Arianna. She could understand their confusion. Moments ago, she'd been reluctant to become an instant mom.

The officer's eyes narrowed. "This is not a competition, ma'am. The children's welfare is at stake."

How come nobody cared about her welfare when she'd been a child? Arianna squared her shoulders. No point in being bitter. She'd rather draw compassion from her experience. She softened her voice and rearranged her facial features. "I understand. I'm asking for your help."

The social worker came through. "You need to show that you can provide a stable environment for them. You just stated you travel a lot and don't have a permanent home."

She certainly did. Argh. "I'll get a house and a stable job. In fact, this lodge is available. I know my friend will gladly let us stay here. You can see for yourselves it has plenty of room for the children and a spacious fenced-in yard for them to play in. I can get a slide installed. The security is state-of-the-art here." Maybe she shouldn't have stated the latter. But she knew all too well how important security was. "I have a clean record." She'd walked on the edge of the law sometimes, but they didn't need to know that. "I'm financially secure."

The social worker looked away as if she didn't want to state the obvious. "Your cousin would have an advantage because he's married."

Arianna's mind whirled. Okay. Okay. She needed a permanent job and a respectable husband, not necessarily in that order.

The first one was doable. The second one?

Why did Kieran pop into her mind? He was as respectable as they come with a great reputation in the community. He was as stable as she was... fluid. *And* he seemed to have a crush on her.

Tall, muscular, and surprisingly caring, he was also the first man who'd made her heart race in years, though she'd done her best not to show it. With her lifestyle and messed-up past, she hadn't considered romance with him.

Could she consider a marriage of convenience?

She'd done a lot of reckless things in her life. But could she marry a man she barely knew for the sake of children she'd never met?

THE END

Other books by Alexa Verde

To see an updated list of all my other books or subscribe to my weekly reader newsletter (and get a free ebook as your welcome gift!) visit my page at https://www.subscribepage.com/alexaverdepublishedbooks

Acknowledgments

First of all, thank You to God for putting up with me, and for all the blessings!

A million thanks to you, my readers, for reading my books, for sending me encouragement, and for supporting me.

Thanks to Laura H and Marilee M for helping name the horse and extra thanks to Sarah S. for the information about horses and horse care.

Many thanks to my street team, Alexa's Amazing Readers, and to my beta readers, whom I love to pieces. Special thanks to Trudy, Mary Jane, Sarah, Margaret, Carol, Michaela, Kate, Gail, Virginia, Julie, and MaryEllen for their feedback and help with typo-spotting!

Heartfelt thanks to author Jessie Gussman for coming up with the idea for the Cowboy Crossing series and for helping me so much on the way. Jessie, you make me laugh, you make me smile, and you make the world a better place.

I also thank my wonderful editor, Deirdre, for coming through for me every time.